A Flash Fiction Exchange Between

Methuselah *and the* Maiden

Sixty Stories to While Away the Hours
David Treadwell and Anneka Williams

A Flash Fiction Exchange Between Methuselah and the Maiden
Copyright © 2021 David Treadwell and Anneka Williams

ISBN: 978-1-63381-265-9

Designed and produced by:
Maine Authors Publishing
12 High Street, Thomaston, Maine
www.maineauthorspublishing.com

Printed in the United States of America

Table of Contents

Stories

"Someone's life's work has vanished."

A married man goes to a cocktail party and strikes up a conversation with a married woman. The sparks fly. He cannot stop thinking about her.

Write a story that takes place over breakfast.

Open your dictionary to any random page. Put your finger on any random word on that page. That is the title—or part of the title—of your next story.

There's an old legend that every ten years trees come alive and walk the earth. During a camping trip, you hear a noise and decide to follow it. You then bump into a tree that can talk to you.

You've been seeing this person (male or female, take your pick) for three months. You believe he/she drinks too much, but you really like him/her. You don't want to kill the relationship.

You're walking down the main street of a small college town. You're with your fellow student, an African American from Newark. Suddenly, a pickup truck speeds by with a big American flag waving in the back. The driver puts his head out the window and yells, "Go back to Africa, ni***r!"

Write a fictional story of how the octopus got eight legs, evolving from a basic squid which just had two legs.

Two strangers are caught at the top of a broken roller coaster. A love story ensues.

A boy and his best friend discover an ancient map in their parents' wine cellar.

Write about someone who is observing their own funeral from out of sight.

"She liked to fit people into the world like puzzle pieces."

Pick a person whom you have encountered in the past year and write a story told from their point of view.

"Well, what I find very interesting is..." he began, and she sank into her chair, exhaling quietly and turning her attention to the empty fields outside.

Everyone is born knowing the day they are going to die. Write about a character whose day of death has already passed, but they are not dead.

Someone does something extreme to return a borrowed item from many years ago.

A woman obsessed with thriller novels wonders if the new man in her life is secretly a top-level government spy.

The flat gray of the morning sky matched her mood. For now, she sat at her desk, her eyes often wandering to the wooden rune stave. Today she would do it.

Compose a story using these three random words: chandelier, toothache, bolo tie.

The floor tasted like....

Write a story that takes place in an empty landscape.

A woman is standing in her backyard talking animatedly on the phone.

Tell a story seen through a window in an apartment in New York City.

Other pregnant women craved pickles, fries, and Mexican food. Me? I craved my next door neighbor. He looked me up and down and smiled back, inviting me in.

A lucky charm is found.

It was a hell of a way to die.

Write a story in which the impossible is now possible.

The smell of chocolate.

"There was a ring in his teacup...."

How the hell do these people live like this?

Introductions

In the spring of 2018, I served on a committee at Bowdoin College tasked with selecting students to receive financial stipends for summer internships. First, the student had to find an organization (or company) anywhere in the world that would agree to provide a meaningful summer experience; then the student prepared an application explaining how the internship would advance her/his career goals. It was a win-win proposition. The organization got a smart, hardworking summer employee at no cost; the student got a valuable summer experience designed to help them crystallize their career goals and, not so incidentally, look good on a resumé.

The competition for such internships was stiff, especially for first-year students. I was very impressed with two first-years who were ultimately chosen to receive awards: Juan Magalhaes, a charming dynamo from Brazil, and Anneka ("Ani") Williams, a focused young woman from small-town Vermont determined to make her mark on the world, probably in something related to the environment.

I approached both Juan and Ani after their meetings with the committee to see if they'd like to get together for coffee. They each agreed. Unbeknownst to them, I had an ulterior motive. My wife Tina and I had developed wonderful relationships with Bowdoin students over the years because of our involvement with the Bowdoin Host Family program. I thought it would be a treat to get to know Juan and Ani as they continued to shine at Bowdoin and beyond.

Ani and I quickly discovered three small-world connections during our initial meeting at the Wild Oats Café in Brunswick. Her father had taught with my stepson Andy Barker at the Gailer School, an innovative day school in Middlebury, Vermont, which has since closed. Moreover, both of her parents were at Princeton at the same time as my son David, although they didn't know each other. Finally, Ani is a fine cross-country runner, as is Andy's daughter Emma, and they had heard of each other.

For the last three years, I've had the pleasure of getting to know Ani through meals in Brunswick, trips to Gelato Fiasco, and occasional "how's it going?" meetings and phone calls. I'm a professional writer, and Ani is very interested in writing, so we'd sometimes share our work.

Two summers ago Ani emailed to ask how I got ideas for writing fiction. I confessed that I'd never written fiction. I spent the bulk of my career writing admissions and fundraising materials for colleges and schools around the country, as well as profiles and articles for several college and school alumni magazines. In "retirement," I've focused on writing for newspapers in Midcoast Maine.

During the summer of 2020, I got a text out of the blue from Ani: "Have you ever tried to write flash fiction? Would you like to try it with me?" I allowed as how I hadn't written flash fiction, but that I'd check it out and get back to her. After several more back-and-forth texts, we agreed to give it a try. One person would suggest a prompt; then both of us would write to that prompt; then we'd each provide brief comments on the other's work. We initially agreed to try to write one a week, but since we're both Type A, get-it-down-now sorts, and we were both having a blast, we picked up the pace to the point where we were writing two or three stories a week.

After we'd each written half a dozen stories, we joked that maybe we should put our work together in a book at some point. We stopped for a breather after writing thirty stories each. This book is a product of our efforts. We hope you enjoy reading them as much as we enjoyed writing them.

—*David Treadwell*

I started my 2020 by counting shooting stars on a backpacking trip in Chilean Patagonia. As we lay gazing at the bright constellations, we shared what we were looking forward to in the coming year and the intentions we had. I was excited for a summer conducting climate change research in Alaska and hoped to savor my last fall in Maine as a Bowdoin College student by watching the sunrise on the coast once a week, taking classes with some of my favorite professors, and exploring the surrounding Maine outdoors. When the COVID-19 pandemic changed our realities in early 2020, it was initially difficult to know how to respond. I remember thinking that quarantine would only last a few weeks, then a month, before I finally settled into the reality that I had absolutely no idea how long it would last.

I spent most of spring and summer 2020 in Mad River Valley, Vermont, with my family. While living at home at age twenty was not something I ever thought I would choose, our family time together proved to be one of the greatest gifts I could have asked for. From gardening to walking in the woods to hiking on local trails to exploring the woods behind our house to swimming in the river every day to long dinners on our patio, my family felt deep gratitude for our home and the simple, everyday routines we developed together.

When I learned that Bowdoin College would be offering courses remotely for the fall of 2020, I felt a pang of sadness at the loss of my college fall, but also a burst of excitement at the prospect of being able to get creative with how I approached my senior year of college. After several serendipitous conversations with friends, I had pieced together the plan of driving from Vermont to Washington State, where I would start my semester living with a small group of friends. While driving out and settling into Washington, my road trip companion introduced me to the concept of "flash fiction." I was intrigued.

I've always loved writing and also been a little terrified by its infinite possibilities and its ability to completely suck you into the craft. Flash fiction seemed like a good way to dive into writing across a range of topics and in a range of styles, but I wanted a partner. I met David Treadwell—a Bowdoin College alumnus— during my first year of college. He has become a mentor and friend, someone I turn to for advice, and someone who is always willing to answer my questions about what Bowdoin was like "back in the day." As he was a professional writer, I was curious what he knew about flash fiction, so I reached out to him. It was as new to him as to me, and we decided to try a flash fiction "exchange" so we could learn with and from each other.

I started the flash fiction project in Washington State, but I carried it with me through a meandering road trip back through the Rocky Mountain West in early October on my way back to Vermont; it was a part of my time spent at my grandfather's house on Great Pond Lake in Belgrade, Maine; and it provided good fodder for dinner table conversations with my parents when our work- and school-from-home lives proved rather routine.

I certainly could not have foreseen the 2020 that came to be as I watched the stars in the Patagonia sky in the early hours of January 1, 2020, but it ended up being a formative and exciting year in a multitude of unexpected ways. And I'm excited that all the uncertainty of 2020 created the opportunity to work on this flash fiction project with David.

—Anneka Williams

A Few Words on Flash Fiction

Flash fiction is a writing medium in which a writer uses a short prompt to craft a brief enclosed story from five to 1,500 words.

How We Worked Together

We agreed that one of us would suggest a prompt and then each of us would write a short story to that prompt. The person suggesting the prompt could either make it up or find one on the internet. Each of us took both approaches.

We would each send our story to the other person, but the other person wouldn't read it until she/he had completed her/his own story.

After we'd each completed our stories and read the other person's stories, we'd write a brief commentary on the other person's work (e.g., "I especially liked it when..." or "I didn't understand..."). We took turns suggesting prompts.

We originally thought we'd try to write one story a week, but our mutual enthusiasm led to a faster output. At our peak, we were writing three or four stories a week.

One

"Someone's life's work has vanished."

Ani

The Adobe House

The news feed of my phone cast a pale glow on my face in the darkness of the room. I read titles without really taking them in as I sat hunched over my kitchen table, waiting for the sun to rise. Just another sleepless night...

As day broke, I ambled out to our patio. The rocks cooled the soles of my bare feet, and a smile etched my lips as I remembered hand-laying the stones with him—New Mexico's sun had rarely felt more intense as we hauled stones back and forth, but the day had ended with cold beers on the new patio outside of our small, adobe home. My face slackened as the memory faded.

I walked back inside, put on water for tea, and gazed around our home...could I still call it that? Everything was tinged with memory. The couch that he had found at an antique store, the clay pot I had made during an intro pottery class in downtown Santa Fe, a bookshelf stocked with our favorites, the desk he had written the majority of his novels from...I sighed as I returned to the kitchen to pour my cup of Earl Grey.

My life wasn't ending...not physically, at least, but now, at sixty-seven, I felt lost...a deep chasm was opening up inside me as I felt my life's work slipping into memory.

I met him when I was twenty-four and he was twenty-five. Friends set us up. And to think that I almost blew him off! We spent two years courting each other while he finished his MFA in creative writing at the Iowa Writers' Workshop, and I ran the outdoor education program for Albuquerque Academy. During those years our relationship evolved through letters, which are currently stored in a box by my bedside. We didn't know for sure we would end up together, but we both quickly discovered that we were hard-pressed to find someone we wanted to share our lives with more than each other and so, upon his MFA completion, we decided to give us a shot. This took the form of driving from New Mexico to Alaska over the course of a fall season, spending a winter skiing at Revelstoke while working night jobs and writing in our free time, and finally settling down in Santa Fe, where he became a locally successful author focusing on creative nonfiction centered on the American Southwest, and I started a small nonprofit focused on providing equal access to wilderness spaces while continuing to run the outdoor education program at Albuquerque Academy.

Kids weren't in the cards for us. While he would never have used these words, it *was* my fault. My body just couldn't handle it. There was a year of sadness and a feeling of loss, but our love never wavered, and we got through it, finding fulfillment in other ways. Our property in Santa Fe started as a classic American Southwest adobe house nestled in the outskirts of town near the base of Atalaya Mountain. Over the years our house took the place of a child. We planted apple and peach trees in our yard, close to the kitchen window. Every four years or so we repainted our door, cycling through shades of blue that made us happy. I could constantly be found tending my flower garden, making arrangements to give away to friends and to brighten up our kitchen table. He was usually at his desk, glancing out the window into our evolving backyard as he thought and wrote and revised. Or he was creating in other ways—building a new outdoor table for us, trimming back the fruit trees, building a trellis for our blossoming vine plants. Our days were long in the best way...full of thought, projects, shared dinners where we balanced musings on the meaning of life and the state of the world with goofy games, jokes, and intermittent silences where we would just appreciate each other's company and enjoy the homestead we had worked so hard to create.

I think the purpose of life is to *find* purpose in life for yourself. In my youth I had thought this would mean a prestigious job, a large home, and a sizable retirement account. But as I was faced with decisions after college, I found the most meaning in more simple things: sharing my love of the outdoors with coming-of-age students at the Albuquerque Academy, spending countless nights camping under the stars as I explored wilderness areas across the country and the world, and building a relationship and home with him...a person who slowed time down for me, who made my stomach hurt from laughing, who continued to give me butterflies even forty years after we first met, and who challenged me in the best of ways.

I lost him a month ago to colon cancer. The end came quickly so there wasn't much time for our life to change; it was just over. I'm getting older, too. Tomorrow I move into town to live with a friend who was also recently widowed. My life isn't over, but some days recently it's felt like it. Am I too old to start a new search for meaning? Was I foolish to think that purpose and meaning weren't just as transient as life itself?

David

It's All in the Cards

M y tale of woe began in a dentist's chair in 1952 when I was ten years old. Mind you, it wasn't about some guy rooting around in my mouth with a sharp pick or drilling me with a miniature sledgehammer. It was about baseball.

I told the dentist that I liked playing Little League baseball, so he told me all about major league baseball while he was rooting and drilling. How there were two leagues and eight teams in each league and how they played 154 games a year and how the winners of each league played in the World Series every fall. I was fascinated. I asked the dentist if he had a favorite team, and he did, and it was the Cleveland Indians, so I decided right then that I'd be a Cleveland Indians fan.

Topps baseball cards had just come out the year before, which was a big deal for boys like me. You got one card and one piece of bubble gum with each purchase (a nickel apiece, as I recall). The card showed a player on the front and all his lifetime statistics, year by year, on the back. You hoped you got a different player with every purchase; if you didn't you would trade it with your friends for a player you didn't have. You were thrilled if you got a player from your team (in my case, the Indians) or a card of a famous player like

Mickey Mantle or Willie Mays because those cards had more trading value.

I kept buying and trading baseball cards all through elementary school and junior high school and high school and college and even well into my adulthood. It became addictive. My collection grew and grew. I tried to get complete sets of a team (the 1956 Indians or the 1961 Yankees and so on). In fact, I tried to get every card that came out in a given year, no mean feat. I had several card-collecting pen pals from around the country and traded with them. I filled shoe boxes at first, and then began putting them in sheets protected with cellophane which I placed in fancy binders. Everything was carefully catalogued.

I collected and collected, well into my fifties when the internet came out, and then eBay started and it became less rewarding, too much like a business. It had been more fun back in the day when a friend and I would just sit there on a warm summer afternoon trading cards and admiring our respective collections and talking about what player we wanted to get next. So I stopped collecting and just put them all away in a big trunk in the basement.

Every now and then when something was going wrong with my career as an accountant or when things were extra tense with my wife, I'd take a couple of cold beers and go down to the basement to pore over my massive baseball card collection, stopping every now and then to reflect upon how I got this or that card. It was calming, like spending a week at a Buddhist retreat or taking a long walk in the woods or a big sip of a good scotch.

Then—yes, it's a cliché—I had a midlife crisis named Joanne; she lived a few towns over and, sure enough, karma crashed the party and my wife Carla found out while I was on a business trip in Chicago. I don't know how she found out, but it didn't matter. Her icy expression when I came home suggested that something bad was up, and I knew what it was, and I knew that I'd better lie low until things got back to more nearly normal.

I went down to the basement to call Joanne and regroup before trying to catch whatever Carla was going to throw at me. I went over to my baseball card trunk for comfort and it was gone, not a trace, gonzo, kaput.

Carla wouldn't have done that now, would she, could she? She had a mean streak, sometimes, but nothing like this. No wife—no matter how badly treated or cheated upon—would ever stoop this low. I walked slowly upstairs and Carla was standing at the top of the stairs, her face beet red, looking half angry and half terrified.

I didn't say anything about the trunk because I didn't want her to know that I knew it was gone. Because that would have led to a fight about my affair and, well, it was just easier to say nothing. So I said nothing. And she said nothing about the affair because she knew that that would lead to a fight about my missing trunk. We were at a stalemate, a steely stalemate.

In fact, we both felt guilty and we were both relieved not to have to face the music—mine about having the affair, hers about pitching my baseball card collection (assuming she did that).

Then the strangest thing happened. I called Joanne and told her the affair was over. Carla and I started to communicate with each other. Really share. And really listen. The walls came tumbling down. I decided that losing my card collection wasn't that big a deal. To every thing a season, they say. Carla apparently decided that my affair was a one-time thing and that I wasn't such a horrible guy after all.

The years passed by and it was almost like the baseball card/affair event had given us new life, a new marriage. For our fiftieth wedding anniversary, our two sons surprised us with a gift certificate for a cruise to Alaska. I gave Carla a certificate promising that she and I would spend time together, just us two, for one weekend a month. No friends. No family. Just us. And, as a bonus, I promised not to be on the computer at all for three nights a week. Those gifts hit the mark. She gave me a week-long fishing trip to Montana. Yes!

And then she said there was one more thing, something that might help me fill my time when I wasn't on the computer. Down in the corner of the basement. Puzzled, I went down to the basement. And there it was. My trunk full of baseball cards. She had given it to her good friend Alice (who knew the whole story) for safekeeping all these years.

That, let me say, was a home run.

Two

A married man goes to a cocktail party and strikes up a conversation with a married woman. The sparks fly. He cannot stop thinking about her.

Ani

Fairy Lights

The stickiness characteristic of lemonade coated the back of my throat as I tossed back my Tom collins, my wedding ring clacking against the glass as I tipped it upward. Across the veranda I heard my wife's tinkling laughter and glanced up just in time to see the people gathered around her lean in eagerly. They were as enamored with her as I had been our sophomore year of college. I snorted into my drink. My wife certainly knew how to charm. She pulled you in...and then she trapped you.

As I stared down into the dregs of my Tom collins, I caught movement out of the corner of my eye. A woman—around my age—was picking her way through the cocktail tables toward me. "Someone next to you?" she asked in a voice surprisingly deep for her small size. I shook my head. She sank into the chair next to me. She was slight but upon second look clearly quite strong. And I noticed her dress—it didn't look uncomfortably tight like those of most of the women in the room, it wasn't an ungodly bright color, and it didn't have even a hint of sequins or glitter or sheen. It was a simple, subtle blue, and it hung loosely around her small frame. I liked it; it conveyed a quiet confidence.

I went back to staring at my empty drink...contemplating a second but also hoping my wife would come and tell me it was time to leave. I wasn't thrilled at the prospect of heading back to our perfectly manicured home, but I just wanted life to speed up...maybe it would get better?

"Look at the way the fairy lights sparkle." I glanced toward the woman next to me who was gazing at the lights twining their way up the posts supporting the veranda's cover. I stared, too. "They're missing out," the woman said, inclining her head toward the crowd around my wife. I stared at this woman. Did she mean seeing the lights? Life?

She nodded toward two men standing in the corner whispering. "What do you think they're talking about?"

I looked up. I hadn't even noticed them. I stared for a second. "Arguing?" I said hesitantly.

"Why do you say that?" she asked.

"Well...they're directly facing each other which seems a little standoffish, neither is smiling, and the one on the left is clenching his hands."

"I'm Amy," the woman said, extending a hand on which I noticed a simple silver band.

The night passed both more slowly and quickly as Amy and I settled into conversation. She made time slow down, maybe because she asked questions and truly seemed to care about the answers. Or was it because she made me look at the world in a way I normally didn't? Despite feeling time slow, I also felt more aware and more engaged.

I was snapped out of my reverie when my wife came to tell me she was tired and ready to go home. Midnight already? Where had the time gone? Amy and I exchanged cordial good-byes, and I watched her walk to her car, get in, and drive away.

The next morning I woke up early and lay in bed listening to the birds chirping outside the window. I felt my wife stir next to me as I gingerly slipped out of the bed. I puttered around the kitchen as the sun rose outside the window. I noticed how the blue fruit bowl bounced incoming sunlight around the kitchen and watched the kids next door playfully jostle each other as they walked down to catch the school bus.

I felt the urge to whistle as I grabbed my keys from the bowl in the mudroom and quietly shut the door behind me so as not to wake my wife. Today was going to be a good day. I was off to buy some fairy lights.

David

A Job for the Boys

He hated these things. Cocktail parties. A lame excuse for drunks to drink. A blizzard of banalities, signifying nothing. Screw it. Only an hour left. Gotta do something as the wife is engrossed in conversation with that woman she says she despises, but whatever.

Suddenly he spots a woman he's never met over in the far corner. Looks interesting. He maneuvers over to her, stands right in front of her and says, "What book are you reading right now?"

The woman: "How do you know I'm even reading a book right now What kind of a man asks a question like that of a woman he's never met?"

Man: "A man who's tired of making small talk with empty people."

Woman: (pauses, smiles) "Fair enough. I'm reading *The Overstory*, by Richard Powers. Have you read it?"

Man. (To himself. *Bingo. I've met my match*.)

The man and the woman spent the next forty-five minutes talking about books and politics and religion. And boring cocktail parties. He felt himself come alive for the first time in weeks, months, maybe years. Here's a woman who gets me. A smart woman. And, in her way, incredibly sexy. Sexy because she gets right to the point and says, in effect, "Here I am. There you are. Who are you? I want to know." She's married, but so what.

The man is lying in bed later that night thinking about that woman and what happened.

(TIME OUT: We interrupt this story to bring in two new characters, the Idster and the Boy Scout. They begin to take turns whispering into the man's ear.)

Idster: Hey, she's yours if you want her. All yours. You saw the way she was hanging on every word. Go for the gold!

Boy Scout: Cool it. She's married. You're married.

Idster: This is 2020. Who knows what tomorrow will bring? Seize the moment!

Boy Scout: Why ruin your life for a quick roll in the hay?

Idster: C'mon man. Look at all those young college kids these days who have something they call "friends with benefits." They just use each other's bodies for a few minutes. Nobody's the wiser. Everybody wins. Maybe she can be your friend with benefits.

Boy Scout: You're not a college kid. You're a grown man. A respected member of the community. You have a wife. You have a good job. You have other responsibilities. Sure, it was a good chat, but leave it at that. Move on.

Idster: Hey, man. You loved being with that woman. Did you get her number? I hope you got her number. What's the worst that could happen?

Boy Scout: Don't do it. Forget it. You'd probably had too many drinks. She probably had too. Stop right now.

Then, suddenly, another character enters the story. The Judge. He pushes aside the Idster and the Boy Scout and begins talking directly to the man.

The Judge: Okay, you've both made good points, but I've made my decision. You got the woman's number. But don't call her. It could turn out to be perfectly harmless, but you just don't know. Put that memory in the memory bank. Use her for fantasies, if you must, but take it no farther.

The man hears the verdict, clenches the pillow, sighs and tries to get some sleep. It takes a long, long time.

Three

Write a story that takes place over breakfast.

Ani

Raspberry Waffles

When Mom wasn't looking, I drizzled more syrup over my waffles. I almost didn't get away with it but managed to quickly place the pitcher of syrup next to the bowl of raspberries before Mom put the paper down. Her face was revealed just long enough for her to take a sip of her coffee..yuck! ...before her face was once again blocked by the crinkly, thin paper.

I watched with glee as the syrup filled the wells of the waffles and used my fork to coax it along until every indent was filled. Next I reached for the bowl of raspberries, snatching up a handful and carefully placing one raspberry in each cell on the waffle's surface. Syrup oozed out of the wells as I pushed the raspberries in, and I sat back, admiring my masterpiece of sugary sweet goodness.

I picked up the fork from the table next to my plate and carefully fit my small hand around it as I'd been taught. I stabbed a corner of the waffle with my fork, ripping off a small chunk. As the ridges between the wells ripped apart, syrup dripped out onto my plate. I smeared my waffle bite in the syrup and began to maneuver it to my mouth.

Just then the paper crinkled, and Mom's head reappeared from behind. She looked at my plate and then glanced at her watch. "Stop playing with your food; it's time to go to school."

David

Love Over Easy

There they sat at the breakfast table, the old man and the old woman, nearing their nineties, still getting out of bed in the morning, still moving around a bit, well beyond their "use by" date. Their kids were gone, their finances were sufficient, their health was okay, all things considered.

The woman looked up from her half-eaten oatmeal and asked softly, "Do you love me?"

"What?" her husband grumbled, a common complaint since his hearing was going and he was used to tuning out his wife most of the time.

"Do you love me?" she repeated more loudly with a tinge of desperation.

"Can we talk about this after breakfast?" asked the man, not wanting to "get into the pit" as he called any conversation that dipped the slightest bit below the surface.

"Please listen to me. Do you love me?"

The man stopped, put down his paper, and pulled back his chair.

"What do you think?" he asked. "We've been married sixty-five years. Raised three kids. Survived your cancer and my bankruptcy. We still have a few friends. We don't totter around drooling. And I manage to remember to zip up my fly, most of the time."

The woman reached over and put her wrinkled hand on his. "I know all that, but that's not what I asked. I want to know. I need to know. Do you still love me?

The man took a long deep breath and looked at his wife. He remembered, in a flash, how they met and when they first kissed and the birth of their first child. He remembered their spats about money and her mother and his father. He remembered some of their camping trips, like the time they had to climb in the car to avoid a bear. And as he reviewed all these memories he felt himself become relaxed, and he eased into the moment, He felt a real warmth welling up inside. He looked over at her and sensed the tears forming in his eyes.

"Yes. I still love you."

"Good," she said, and went back to her oatmeal.

Four

Open your dictionary to any random page. Put your finger on any random word on that page. That is the title—or part of the title—of your next story.

Ani

Pure Bunkum

I sniff the air...bacon? Leaping off my bed, I bound downstairs, wagging my tail furiously. My humans are just sitting down. I sit next to the littlest human, knowing she'll slip me something from the table when the big humans aren't looking. I don't have to wait long before a glistening, greasy piece of bacon drops onto the floor in front of my nose. I inhale it and then look up...more?

I sit impatiently under the table, beating my tail to remind the humans that I'm still here. When the little human is finished (sadly, she didn't share any more of her bacon with me), she heads for the door, and I eagerly spring up and follow. I accidentally trip her as we both try to squeeze through the door at the same time, but I lick her face as she gets up to let her know I'm sorry.

Fresh air! I grab my frisbee and race a few laps around the yard. So many good smells—squirrels, bacon, human sweat, grass...what's that sound? I prick my ears up then race to the road. More humans coming to my house! Another little human gets out of the car, followed by a big human who...ugh what is that smell? It's strong and kind of like flowers maybe? But not real flowers, flowers that smelled like chemicals. Yuck! Did this woman purposely bathe herself in such a strong smell? I go over to sniff the big human, then I rub against her legs, hoping she'll pet me. I get a light pat on the head and I know immediately this is *not* my type of human. This is one of those humans who pretends to like dogs but could not be more fake about it. These humans tend to be glued to these shiny boxes that glow and ring and vibrate. These humans tend to spend most of their time inside, don't like it when I try to cuddle after coming in from outside, and talk down to me in high-pitched, screeching voices like I'm some idiot creature. I avoid these humans at all costs.

I sit down, far away from the chemically flower-scented big human, waiting for her to leave. The little humans have run off together, though, and the big human is not leaving but instead walking into my house. I bound ahead of her. She shies away from me as I race past her, giving a little gasp. I wag my tail to indicate I didn't mean to scare her, but she does not look happy.

This new big human settles into the table at our house and, sure enough, she sits at the table and pulls out her glowing metal box while one of my big humans gets water for her. I settle onto my bed, glowering at her. She is invading my home and taking the attention of my humans. The two big humans sit at the table, talking. Normally I like listening to my humans talk. Their voices sound happy and passionate. I like hearing them laugh, I like the silences that feel full of thought, I like the deep rumbling voice of the biggest human compared to the high voice of the little human. I do not like listening to this new human talk, though. She talks so fast and so loud that it grates on my ears, and I pull them close to my head to try to dampen the noise. Despite seeming to have a lot to say, there's no passion in her voice. It's very flat. And there are no silences. Does she even have time to think about what she's saying? Probably not.

I try to go to my happy places—romping outside with *my* humans, the time they gave me a bone with meat on it, kicking up fallen leaves on the ground, running through the cold white sand we have during some parts of the year, getting a belly rub, napping by the fire when it's cold out, sleeping next to my little human every night and waking her up with kisses in the morning...but I can't focus; the flat voice of the new human continues to grate on my ears.

I put my chin down on my bed and growl softly in the back of my throat, resigning myself to the fact that I'm just going to have to lie here and listen to this fake human prattle on without expressing any passion or depth. Pure bunkum.

David

Normality Takes a Day Off

Silas Brown was the kind of man who knew what he wanted and wanted what he knew. He lived alone so there was no one around to throw his schedule off track. Same breakfast every day at eight sharp (Kellogg's Corn Flakes, toast with grape jam, and coffee). Same duties at his accounting office every day. Same conversations with his equally anal assistant Myrtle. After work, it was dinner at six o'clock sharp. Pork chops on Monday. Spaghetti (canned) on Tuesday. And so on. Then watch television for three hours before going to bed at ten.

One Saturday morning he got up at the usual seven o'clock sharp time, but things soon began to go wrong. There was no coffee in the cupboard. That would never do. So he got in his old Corvair and headed for the store. He was already running late. (Yes, it was a Saturday but schedules still needed to be followed) so he drove faster than usual, much to the delight of the policeman who pulled him over for going forty-seven miles an hour in a thirty-five-mile-an-hour zone. Mr. Brown had never had a ticket before.

Now Mr. Brown was really flustered. When he went to the register to pay for the coffee with his credit card, he put an Amazon gift card into the machine by mistake. *Will this day never end?* he wondered.

Driving home he was careful not to speed, but then speeding was no longer an issue when four turkeys began crossing the road right in front of him. Now Mr. Brown started huffing and puffing. He had never had a day like this.

After his late breakfast, he went out to take his walk, one hour after he normally would do on a Saturday morning. Small problem. For a widow, Mrs. Fiddlebottom, happened to be walking by his house and asked if she could join him on his walk. *Well, the day has already gone crazy*, thought Mr. Brown. So he said, "Yes."

Mrs. Fiddlebottom began asking lots of questions, just to get a conversation going. Mr. Brown gave her lots of short answers like "Yes" or "No," but he began boring even himself. So he started expanding on the answers and having a real conversation with a real exchange of thoughts and feelings.

At the end of the walk, Mrs. Fiddlebottom said shyly, "That was fun, Silas. May I call you Silas? Mr. Brown seems so formal since we're practically neighbors and all. Would you like to walk together again tomorrow?"

Mr. Brown stopped for a minute to think about whether his normal Sunday schedule including a morning walk. It didn't. What would he do? *Well, why not?*, he thought. This wasn't so bad. And being with Mrs. Fiddlebottom made him feel better then he usually did.

"Yes," said Mr. Brown." I will see you tomorrow at this exact same time. I like to stay on a regular schedule. Mostly."

Five

There's an old legend that every ten years trees come alive and walk the earth. During a camping trip, you hear a noise and decide to follow it. You then bump into a tree that can talk to you.

Ani

The Boat Builder's Granddaughter

The soughing of the wind in the canopy of birch trees above me was both eerie and strangely comforting. A strong wind whipped my face as I stood in the clearing facing the edge of the forest. My friends formed a wall behind me, blocking me from the warm glow of our campfire and the comfort of our tents.

"Come on!"

"Don't be a baby!"

"What...scared of the dark?"

I had told them not to mess with the woods, with the trees. My grandfather had been a boat builder, and I had grown up watching him work in his barn, surrounded by slabs of oak. Witnessing him turn whole trees into sleek, seaworthy vessels was akin to magic. "Trees and wood are powerful," he had always said. And he had always respected the trees, never taking any wood that hadn't naturally fallen. Maybe I was silly for believing him...but then again, this would be the tenth year since the last Awakening...if the myth was true, of course.

And now I had to face the woods because I had stupidly told my friends that my grandfather believed trees came alive and spoke to people every ten years, oh and by the way, this was one of those years.

"You *cannot* be that gullible!"

"Come on, how is that even possible?"

"You actually believe the trees come alive every ten years, don't you?"

It had taken almost everything I had not to point out that trees were, in fact, living beings in response to that last piece of ridicule. I don't know what I had expected, it probably *was* just a silly myth. But why did I feel so scared to face the woods? It had always been my happy place, a place for adventures, a place to just think, and, recently, an escape from the superficial world of college parties, boys, and the stress of finding my place in the world.

I faced the birch trees swaying in the wind, pulling my fleece tighter around me. I willed myself not to look back at my friends as I stepped out of the yellow glow of our firelight and into the darkness of the forest.

I blinked as my eyes adjusted to the blackness. The crunch of my steps seemed to punch the quiet air—mid-October and already the forest floor was littered with shed leaves. *Twenty minutes*, I thought. *All you have to do is spend twenty minutes in here, that's all your friends want. You can do it.*

I settled myself against the base of a large oak, breathing in the familiar scent of my grandfather's boat barn and letting the cool night air settle over me. I breathed in for four counts and then out for four counts, in four, out four, in four, out four...

A sudden warmth began in the middle of my spine despite the chill of the air. I jumped up quickly as it got hotter. The tree was...glowing? I laid my hand against the rough bark of the trunk and, in an instant, my mind wasn't just my own. My memory snapped back to the time I was eight and running through the woods and had sprawled after tripping on a low line of barbed wire; then I was ten and watching the forest next to my school be chopped down to make room for our new tech building; then I was thirteen and learning about increasing atmospheric carbon dioxide and the deforestation of the Amazon rainforest; then I was sixteen and knocked over by a wave of sadness and loss as I visited the only Dutch elm tree in my county to survive the *O. ulmi* invasion that had wiped out the rest of the population. My memory was out of control. It was as if I were a spectator in my own mind as some other force hurtled me through a series of specific experiences from my past. Now I was eighteen and walking in the woods after the first snowfall of the winter, admiring the ice-encased branches and marveling at the sun sparkling off the fresh layer of snow. And suddenly it was last year...I was twenty years old and sitting in a plant ecophysiology lecture learning about the particulars of California redwood survival and marveling at the ability of trees to push up against their physiological limits of evolution. Just as quickly as the warmth had begun, it ended, and I was once again the only thing in my mind. I peered through the darkness at the oak tree... noticing the deep ridges and rough texture of its bark. I glanced at my watch; my twenty minutes were up.

My friends got up from the fire as I reappeared from the woods.

"You actually did it!"

"Talk to any trees?"

"So, was the myth true? Did any trees come alive?"

Someone had once told me that most people's eyes flicked up and to the left when they told a lie. "My grandfather is just a silly old man," I said, forcing my eyes to stare straight ahead.

David

A Talk in the Woods

I needed this camping trip, some time alone, away from everything and everyone. No real estate deals to put together. No arguments about curfew times with my teenage daughter Becky or driving privileges with my teenage son Randy. No blaring headlines about the latest outrage in Washington or the latest scandal in Sacramento. A visit north, up near Mill Valley sounded perfect. I had decided to skip the Muir Woods National Monument, the site of the massive redwoods and hordes of overweight Midwesterners, birdwatching seniors, and camera-laden Japanese tourists, and find a secluded spot about ten miles east of the park.

On the first morning, I got up early to take a hike in the fog before breakfast. Suddenly, through the mist, I spotted this huge tree, about twenty feet wide and Lord knows how tall, springing up from the ground toward the sky. It can't be a redwood, I thought, this far from the monument. And there were no other giant redwoods around.

As I neared the mammoth tree, I heard a deep booming voice say, "Hi, there. What is your name?"

What the hell! Am I dreaming?

"Is there a person hiding behind that tree? Speak up! Come out!"

"No. It's just me. Big Red. A big ole redwood tree. Today's my two hundredth birthday, but you don't need to give me any presents. Just sit down and chat a spell. That would be a great present."

I hadn't been drinking and I hadn't been smoking, and I hadn't been known to hallucinate, so I thought, what the hell, just go with it, and leaned back against the tree.

"So what have you been doing for the last two hundred years, Big Red?"

"Good question," the tree replied, "long answer, but I'll just give the highlights. Back in the 1840s when I was just a youngster, a bunch of men from the East came to California looking for gold. You've probably heard of the Gold Rush. They were crazy. Drank a lot. Cussed a lot. Went whoring around a lot; that's what they said, anyway.

"And then around 1900, there was that huge fire in San Francisco that we could see from all the way up here. That was downright scary! Lots of fires happening these days, too, but they protect the National Monument pretty well, and besides, we redwoods are fairly immune to normal forest fires.

"And then in the mid-1900s using redwood to build houses became the big thing. I lost a lot of friends during that craze. Happily, we're protected now."

Big Red paused to take a breath—even trees need to breathe—so I asked him another question. "How did you happen to be here, away from all the other redwood trees?"

"Well," he said, "every ten years we trees get this special power to move around if we want to. Most of the other redwood trees don't bother because they're pretty old and tired. Also, they seem to like getting their pictures taken. I just needed a break this time, so I came over here for a while; then I'll go back to where I belong. No one ever comes out this way, but then you showed up. By the way, why didn't you just go to Muir Woods where all the other people go with their fancy cameras and their loud noises and everything?"

"I guess I'm like you," I answered. "I needed to get away too, off the beaten path. I always wondered what trees would say if they could talk, and now I know. Or at least I know what you would say. It's been real nice chatting with you, Big Red."

"Yes, it has," admitted the redwood. "It's good to know that at least one person is interested in more than a photo op when they see a tree like me. I hope we can get together again in ten years, deal?"

"Deal," I said; then headed back to the campsite. This was going to be a very good day.

Six

You've been seeing this person (male or female, take your pick) for three months. You believe he/she drinks too much, but you really like him/her. You don't want to kill the relationship.

Ani

I Love Him, I Love Him Not

I really like this boy. He's cute, kind, funny, goofy, endearingly awkward. He makes me laugh, he gives me butterflies even now, three months into seeing each other. I love that we can bounce from deep, philosophical conversations to silly games or crude humor. He asks about my family. It feels easy to spend time together. I've never felt this way about anyone. But... no, don't go there. You're being silly, you're overthinking it. Do you *really* think he has a drinking problem? Well...he does drink a lot. But it doesn't affect me *that* much. What about that time? No, you're being ridiculous. Would he get mad if I said something? What if we can't actually learn how to fight? What if it ends the relationship? He likes you, you like him. It's meant to be. No, of course I don't believe in "the one." But I do *really* like him. The drinking is just a minor issue, right? I could totally address it once we have a more established relationship. He could change. He probably knows it's a problem...right? We're young, he'll outgrow it! I don't think I should say anything. Not yet. I can live with it. It can't be that bad, right?

David

A Fork in the Road

We were at Alonzo's, our favorite Italian restaurant in the East End. And then what happened was what always happened. Connie wanted to order a bottle of Malbec, our favorite wine. I suggested we each order just a glass and call it even. She relented, and then, sure enough, she drank her glass faster than I did, and then she asked for another. And another. And another. She had been right, money wise, in the first place; it would have been cheaper to buy a whole bottle. But that wasn't the point, and I knew it. And maybe she did too. I'd seen this movie before.

We began dating three months ago, thanks to a lucky hit on Hey, Cupid. We connected right away; everything clicked. We shared the same views on books (nonfiction), movies (independent), music (classical), sports (Go, Sox!) and politics (Dump Trump). I was in my early forties and beginning to think I'd never find Miss Right. She was in her late thirties, very smart, very successful, very attractive—and very reluctant, she told me, to settle for just anyone.

She laughed a few days later when she told me that she had cancelled her next three Hey, Cupid dates after meeting me. We both felt like we had won the lottery. And in the most important ways we had. The courtship continued at warp speed. We found out that we both wanted two kids (ideally one girl and one boy), and we both wanted to retire at age sixty and go travel. Except....except for her tendency to drink too much when we went out to eat. Or when we didn't. One glass always became more than one and then more than that. I didn't like who she became when she got tipsy (her word) or sloshed (mine).

I'd never said anything beyond suggesting that she and I might cut back on the drinking a little. She always got bristly at the suggestion, so I'd drop it. But something told me I could no longer just "drop it." And that something was my mother.

My dad and mom had had a long painful struggle with drinking for most of their marriage, if you could call it a marriage. They both went to AA and quit drinking. But then she started to drink again, secretly, at first, but then out in the open. My dad got tired of arguing about it; he figured that it was her life. But it wasn't just her life. It was all our lives—his, hers, mine, my two younger brothers'. Then she went to sleep one night when I was in college and never woke up. It was a nightmare, yes, but also a relief—especially for my dad.

So the morning after the Alonzo dinner we were at the kitchen table having a late breakfast. I said, "We have to talk." She got that stricken look like she sometimes did when the she felt like she'd been put in the penalty box for something. I had said little to her before about my mom and dad's drinking. It was too painful, and I always wanted to put the best spin on everything. But I told her all about it, and left nothing out.

She looked angry at first, then sad, and finally almost blank.

When I finished there was a long pause, a few minutes. She said, "Is that all?" I said it was. Then she said, "Okay, I'll think about it" and left the table.

We had dinner at home that night. She looked beautiful, peaceful, content. Especially when her hand shook just a little as she sipped her Diet Coke.

Seven

You're walking down the main street of a small college town. You're with your fellow student, an African American from Newark, Suddenly, a pickup truck speeds by with a big American flag waving in the back. The driver puts his head out the window and yells, "Go back to Africa, ni***r!"

Ani

The Limits of Wearing Other's Shoes

"F*** you!" I shout at the pickup truck as it speeds by, an American flag trailing off the left bumper. But my words are lost against the revving engine. I turn to Grace; her jaw is clenched and her eyes are steely.

"I...look that..." I trail off, unsure of what to say. There's not really anything I *can* say.

Grace stares ahead, her voice shaking slightly. "Unbelievable. I've never even been to Africa. It's 2020! How could people assume that every black person is from Africa. I just don't get it."

"It's crazy, I know."

"No, you don't," Grace snaps at me. And she begins to accelerate.

It's true. I don't get it. I can sympathize but I will never understand on a fundamental level what it feels like to be a black person in America. I think back to elementary school. My friend Emily once asked, "If you peel the skin off everyone, we look the same underneath, right?" While that now sparks a horrifying image akin to reading a Stephen King novel, I can't help but wonder...

David

Standing Up

W hat were they thinking when they paired Ray and me as roommates for our first year? I'm your basic privileged white kid from Santa Barbara, California. My family goes on fancy vacations. I graduated from a la-di-dah day school. I surfboard, so I have that long blond hair that people from other places think of when they think of California. Sure, I was a good student, but I always tried to hide the fact. Being a good student wasn't cool where I grew up. But it's cool here at this college, which gets smart kids from all over.

Ray, on the other hand, is an inner-city kid. Rough home environment. But very smart and amazing at video games (maybe that's why they paired us up). We talked about why we chose to come here. He was concerned that a small college in Maine wouldn't be a great fit for him, but he visited the campus, and other African American students assured him that things were mainly okay here.

After a few long talks that went well into the night, we really got to know each other. I confessed my anxiety that he would think I was just a spoiled white rich kid. He confessed that he thought that other students would think he just got accepted because he was African American.

In no time, we had broken down the boundaries, but then it happened. A few weeks after the beginning of school, we were walking down Main Street and this redneck asshole in a pickup truck yelled, "Go back to Africa, ni***r!" I couldn't believe it. Neither could Ray. He looked at me with fear and anger flashing in his eyes.

I tried to get a photo of the truck's license plate, but it was too late. It was quickly out of sight. A bystander overheard the whole event and said, "That's the jerk from Lisbon Falls who's always driving around in that pickup truck. Puts this town to shame! Wish I had a gun with me."

"I am so sorry, Ray," I said. "I don't know what to say. I didn't know this town was like that."

"That's okay," said Ray, still visibly shaken. "I've heard that crap before many times. I just didn't expect to hear it here."

We walked slowly back to the campus to decide what to do or who to tell about what happened. We decided to go to the first year dean's office to report the incident. Then we returned to our room for a long talk.

Ray really opened up about how he had come to a small college in Maine to prepare for a better life without fear of being beaten up or shot. I tried to assure him that this was a really rare event, but I knew that it could happen to young men like Ray at any time anywhere. I told him I had his back as best I could. I also said that I would write an article about the incident to send to the college paper and maybe even the town paper.

Ray sensed, I think, that I really felt his pain and sadness. I think that touched him pretty deeply. Maybe he learned a little about me that night. I know I learned a lot more about him. And that was good.

Eight

Write a fictional story of how the octopus got eight legs,
evolving from a basic squid which just had two legs.

Ani

The Fastest Squid

Five hundred million years ago the first fish appeared in the ocean. They were relatively simple—small creatures, not much variation in color, several fins. In fact, these fish resembled those made famous by Dr. Seuss's *One fish, two fish, red fish, blue fish*. And all were equal except for the red squid. Five hundred million years ago, the red squid was king of the ocean (except for the orca whale, of course). The red squid was a rare species—the size of a small sedan, its two legs allowed it to zip around the ocean chasing blue fish (its preferred food source) and following the warm water that it so loved.

Red squid are arrogant creatures, and every year there would be a red squid festival held at a famous kelp forest located off of what are today known as the Galapagos Islands. The festival was a chance for the red squid—of which there were only twelve in the entire ocean—to convene and discuss their territories and vote on who had the longest legs and the reddest mantles. In this particular year, however, a red squid named Arlo, who dominated the section of ocean between Antarctica and Chile, demanded that a speed competition be added to the red squid festival. The other squid laughed at Arlo because Arlo had been born with three legs, rather than two. "You don't actually think you could be faster than us?!" one squid asked. But they agreed to put it to a vote. Arlo nervously twirled his tentacles while the other squid discussed his idea, but ultimately the speed competition passed in a vote of seven to four.

It was decided that the competition would take place on the second-to-last day of the red squid festival. Every squid would have to swim west from the edge of the kelp forest off the Galapagos, around the island that is today known as Hawaii, and then head east back to the Galapagos. The eldest red squid, Alistair, would preside over the competition.

As the squid lined up at the edge of the kelp forest, red, green, and white fish gathered to watch. (Blue fish, as the preferred food of squid, were, of course, nowhere to be found.)

"On your mark, get set, go!"

There was a flurry of bubbles as the eleven red squid in the race furiously started propelling themselves through the water by churning their legs. The squad of squid strung out quickly and soon were lost from view.

Alistair anxiously puttered around the kelp forest awaiting the finishers. He waited three days and two nights before he finally heard a white fish shout "Look! It's Arlo." Sure enough, Arlo, with his three legs waving wildly, was speeding toward the edge of the kelp forest.

As the other squid trickled in they were stunned. Arlo, with his goofy third leg, had just out-swum them all!

The speed competition was a huge success, and over the next hundred million years, it got even more competitive. The red squid started procreating more in the hopes of having children with three or more legs who were guaranteed to perform well in the annual speed competition. And sure enough, seventeen generations after Arlo's first win, the average squid had four legs. Now, not only were these squid better competitors in the speed competition, but they also lived longer because they were better at catching blue fish and evading orca whales.

Year after year the speed competition continued, and every seven generations or so, a red squid family would have a red squid baby with one more leg than was typical in the modern era. However, forty-seven million years ago, a red squid family found themselves with an eight-legged baby that was purple! This purple squid was named Avery, and she quickly discovered that she could blend in with schools of blue fish and catch them more easily, and pretty soon all the red squid wanted to be purple and have eight legs, just like Avery!

Unfortunately, purpleness remained a rare quality. And purple squid, believing themselves superior to red squid, only married other purple squid. When Avery was thirty-seven years old, she tried to go to the annual red squid festival only to find that the red squid had decided that the festival was for red squid and red squid only! In fact, purple squid with eight legs were given a new name—"octopus"—to separate them from red squid. If you're lucky and can vacation in the Galapagos Islands during the red squid festival, it is said that you may be able to catch a glimpse of an octopus spying on the festival from deep within the kelp forest.

David

Frustration in the Kingdom

God was having a bad day. The people on earth, his most intelligent creation, had gone mad. There was plenty of space for everyone, but fights were breaking out all over the world. One tribe always wanted to take over the land of another tribe. There was plenty of food but again, not enough people were willing to share.

"Where did I go wrong?" he mused. "Those people can pray all they want and wring their hands about this and that, but they're the ones who need to make peace. I've done my part. I can't take it anymore right now."

And then, just when God had about given upon the state of humans, he got more bad news from St. Peter. "I hate to interrupt you, God," said St. Peter, "but we have a problem in the cephalopod family. Too many squid are getting eaten by the sharks and the tuna. Soon there won't be any squid left. Do you want to do something about that?"

"Oh, Christ," said God, lapsing into a rare blasphemy. "Give me some time to think about it."

God retired to his chambers to consider what to do about the endangered squid. Then suddenly, the answer came to him. "I've got it! The squid needs another creature to take off some of the heat. And it should be

68

a member of the cephalopod family. I'll create one with eight legs, whereas the poor squid has only two. Eight is a nice number, and besides, the Chinese consider it a lucky number. So that's it. I'll call this new creature an octopus."

So that's how God created a new creature called the octopus. In a short time, the sharks and tuna discovered that octopuses were every bit as tasty as squid. Moreover, they were especially scrumptious for those who loved the tangy taste of cephalopod leg meat.

In a few months, word got around squid nation that this new creature—the octopus—had saved their very future. They banded together to send a thank you note to God, carefully crafted, of course, using squid ink on parchment paper.

Nine

Two strangers are caught at the top of a broken roller coaster. A love story ensues.

Ani

Serendipity

I hated the state fair with my whole heart. I avoided it like the plague. Except for this year, of course. It was my senior year of high school and, just for a day, I wanted to be a normal teenager. So here I was, at the fair with friends, nibbling on big fluffs of maple cotton candy, waiting in line for rides, eyeing boys sporting athletic wear and goofy grins wandering through the crowd...It was *so* not my scene. I longed for a lazy afternoon spent curled up reading in the hammock set up between two trees in the edge of our yard, and I couldn't believe I was passing up an opportunity to work in our garden beside my mom. But, here I was, demonstrating that I could be a normal teenage girl and hating most of it. In fact, I think the only element of the day I was enjoying was the people watching. It was fascinating to see how my friends instantly changed when we approached a group of guys our age. Or to notice differences in how parents, well...parented...their kids: some adopted the leash-the-child so you don't lose it approach, while others hurtled frantically after their offspring as the kids raced through the crowds, seeking out the next big ride.

And now, here I was, stuck at the top of the Zipper. I had managed to make it half the day avoiding all rides, but my friends had caught on and dared me to do one.

The competitive side of me couldn't back down, so here I was, jammed into a box with a guy about my age. As we sat, rocking slightly back and forth in the wind, I felt him looking at me. He had a goofy grin, hair long enough to look windswept from the two minutes of hurtling through the air we'd had before the ride broke, and inquisitive brown eyes.

"This sucks," he said. I glanced over again, startled. He was probably just talking about the ride being broken, right? He probably loved the fair like everyone else our age.

"I hate the fair even when rides work," I offered, figuring I couldn't lose anything by being honest. He smiled, looking surprised.

"I'm only here because I've never been and figured it was an experience one should have," he explained. Whoa, I thought, and looked at him more closely.

"So what would you rather be doing?" I asked.

"Well..." he started, shyly.

Two hours later and we finally were lowered to the ground, the maintenance guy unlocked our door, and we stepped back into the sunlight. I was reeling. Who was this boy—Liam? We lived one town apart but had never overlapped. And now we'd just had a two-hour conversation that changed my life. Liam noticed me, he listened to me, and I didn't feel scared of just being honest and open with him. And he was thoughtful and creative and independent.

"So...hike next week," I confirmed as we each eyed our waiting friends. He smiled and then we turned, each walking back to friends who would talk constantly while saying nothing for the rest of the day. But I was content, because I now knew Liam was out there. Serendipity at its finest, I supposed.

David

Stopped Time

"**B**itch," James muttered to himself, as the roller coaster slowly chugged its way up to the top of a steep incline. He had been at odds with his girlfriend Molly for several days. They'd been going to together for a year, when they decided to share an apartment three months ago. Suddenly, the roller coaster came to a complete stop.

"What happened?" asked the young woman sitting next to him, after a few minutes.

"Dunno," James muttered. "They're probably just letting people off.

"I know," she said, "but it's been longer than usual." Another minute passed.

"Well, when life gives you lemons, make lemonade," she said. "I'm Emily. What's your name."

"My name's Lemon," said James.

"Oh, I didn't mean you were a lemon!' Emily protested, laughing.

James: "I know that; I'm just in a grumpy mood."

Emily: "Did your dog die?"

James: "No, my girlfriend and I haven't been getting along well lately." Pause.

Emily: "I'm sorry to hear that." Long pause. "Would you rather not talk?"

James: "I'm sorry to be so grumpy. Sure, let's talk."

For the next twenty minutes, Emily and James talked. And talked. About James's career as a software engineer. About Emily's as a second-grade teacher. About their mutual interests in theater and the Red Sox. Then James got a text from Molly. "Are you okay? They say it will take at least another hour to fix the roller coaster. Something about getting a part." Jim replied, "I'm fine." He looked down and could see Molly waving at him. A few seconds later Emily got a text from one of her two friends on the ground with the same message. She replied by saying she was okay, that she was talking with a nice guy. A text came right back, "Is he cute?" Molly started answering "ye..." and Jim asked her what she was doing. They both put down their phones and continued their conversation.

They talked about their families—his dysfunctional, hers traditional. They both expressed the desire to have a family someday. Emily confessed that she'd broken up with a guy a few weeks earlier but felt fine about it.

As they talked, James felt his anger melt away. He felt warm, at peace, accepted—a different feeling than he'd been having lately when he was with Molly, a lawyer who, he felt, sometimes put him on the witness stand to defend this or that small transgression. Then he got another text from Molly. He just wrote "fine" and turned off his phone.

After a short pause in their conversation, Jim looked at Emily and, as if by instinct, rubbed her cheek softly with the back of his hand. "You're trouble for me."

"Trouble?" protested, "I haven't done anything."

"You've done a lot," said James, "in helping me better understand who I am and what I want."

"Well, I'm happy I've been able to help," said Emily, just as the roller coaster started moving. The roller coaster whooshed down to the bottom of the ride, at which point Jim blurted, "Can I have your phone number?"

"What about your girlfriend," asked Emily.

"Can I have your phone number," James repeated.

"Sure," said Emily. She wrote it down on a small piece of paper and gave it to James, just as the roller coast was coming to a stop at the end of the ride.

Ten

A boy and his best friend discover an ancient map in their parents' wine cellar.

Ani

A Planet from the Past

Will raced from the window to the door as Emma's mom's red Subaru pulled up to the front of the house. "Emma's here!" he shouted to no one in particular. And it was about time. He'd been restlessly bouncing around the living room waiting for his friend to show up for what felt like years.

Emma and Will escaped upstairs while the parents exchanged the usual pleasantries in the front hall. Will's dad and Emma's mom were both geology professors at the local college and always had lots of catching up to do.

In his room, Will eagerly showed Emma the new model plane he had built the night before. "It's a P-40B Tiger Shark," he said, as Emma zoomed it around the room.

"I bet your dad helped you," she teased.

Will flushed, "Nuh uh."

Emma and Will had been best friends for the whole ten years they had been alive. Neither had many other friends. Will's mom said it was because he was too absorbed in his own projects and fantasy world's. And Emma fit right into Will's world.

"So, what do you want to do?" Emma asked.

"We could play Mastermind," Will suggested.

"No, you always win, and besides, that's your favorite game, not mine. Let's play spy."

Spy was a game that could be played anywhere at any time. And really it wasn't even a game. Will and Emma would creep around, trying to listen in on conversations without being seen, poking through storage spaces looking for old artifacts, and evading "bad guys" who usually took the form of Will's older brother, Jack.

Today, they started by concealing themselves in the hall closet. They took turns peeping through the lighted crack in the door, watching as Will's mom bustled from the laundry room to the bedroom and listening as Jack talked to friends in his room. Will almost gave away their hiding place by gasping as he heard Jack swear at one of his friends through the phone, but Emma quickly clapped a hand over his mouth.

As their legs were starting to ache, Emma suggested they go down to the wine cellar and poke around. The wine cellar was a cement room located off the house's basement. It was hot and cramped. Wine cases lined the walls of the small space.

"Let's pretend that there's one bottle of wine that has a secret message in it," Emma suggested. "We need to split up and look for it." So Will and Emma began pawing through the wine cases, using two hands to carefully lift out bottles of wine and examine the labels for signs of hidden treasure.

Just as Will was moving a wine case out from the wall he saw something flutter to the ground. He stooped to pick it up. "Emma! Look! It's a map." She came rushing over and they pored over the map.

"Whoa," she exclaimed. "It's a different planet!"

"Pal-e-o-zoo-ic Er-a," Will sounded out, reading the lettering across the top of the faded map.

"But wait, some of the names are the same," said Will, pointing to "Antarctica" and "Europe."

"Yeah, but look, there's no 'Gondwana' on Earth," Emma replied, matter of factly. "And the continents don't look like that on Earth—on this planet they're all squished together." Will didn't know how to argue with that.

Emma and Will spread the map out on the floor, fascinated by the faded colors of continents and the weird looking arrangement of land and ocean. They took turns running their fingers along the faded paper, as if touching the map would help them better understand what they were looking at.

Emma stayed for dinner that night, and as the two children sat at the table with Jack and Will's parents, Emma proudly announced that they had discovered a map from another planet in the wine cellar.

"It's probably from a different galaxy, even," Will chimed in.

"Yeah! The name of the map is 'Paleozoic Er-a' which isn't even a planet in our galaxy!"

Will's parents exchanged a knowing smile.

That night as Will settled into bed, he carefully folded the map and tucked it under his pillow. There was no way he was going to risk losing it—he and Emma had just discovered rare documentation of a different planet! And with that thought, he smiled as he drifted off to sleep.

David

Antique Mapquest

"Holy crap!" The sharp curse shattered the tranquil mood of the setting. A small wine cellar tucked in the far corner of a large basement of a majestic colonial in Concord, Massachusetts, on a rainy fall day when exploring a wine cellar held more promise for two nerdy teenagers than battling it out yet again on *Star Wars Jedi: Fallen Order* in the family den upstairs.

David and his best friend Jon had gone down to the basement out of boredom, but when David had pointed to the door of the wine cellar, Jon immediately cried, "Let's check it out!"

David was reluctant at first, because he'd promised his parents that he'd never go in there unless one of them was with him. He had always enjoyed looking at the rows of old wines and asking his parents where they had bought this or that bottle and how much it was worth and why some wines gained in value over the years and others did not.

"Look at this!" said Jon, when he showed David the ancient, yellowed map he had found tucked in a crack of the wall behind the last bottle on the bottom row of wines.

They both stood over the map in awe, wondering how it got there and what it was worth and whether they should tell David's parents about it. They quickly agreed that they would tell no one about it because, after all, they had found the map, and it might be worth a lot of money.

They rushed upstairs to check the web and learn how to determine the value of an old map. After looking on eBay and browsing the sites of map dealers around the US, they arrived at two conclusions: (1) The values of old maps ranged all over the place, from $50 to well into the thousands and, in some cases, much, much more; (2) They needed to talk to someone who really knows about old maps.

"We have to go directly to a dealer," said David, "and get an appraisal or at least some ideas about what we should do."

Their research led to the ideal candidate: Boston Rare Maps in Southampton, Massachusetts. It was only two hours away and, even better, it was close to Amherst College, which both boys ranked high on their prospective college lists. They could tell their parents they wanted to visit Amherst and arrange to go to Boston Rare Maps on the same day.

Their plan worked. A few weeks later they walked into Boston Rare Books, which was located in an old brick building on a side street in Southampton. The man behind the counter was a throwback, right out of a Dickens novel. Balding head. Thick sideburns. Round spectacles. "How can I help you?"

"I'm David Collins," David explained. "I live in Concord, and I had called you to see if you would look at an old map we have and assess its value or at least suggest what we might do with it."

"Oh, yes," said the man, whose name, Herman Crossbranch, fit his appearance. "Let me take a look."

The man studied the map through a gold-rimmed loupe for a few minutes and then looked up at the boys.

"Where did you get this?" he asked, his voice barely above a whisper.

"We found it," answered Jon.

"Where?" pressed the man. The boys looked at each other nervously.

"In my parents' wine cellar," said David, "in a crack in the wall behind one of the bottles at the bottom of a shelf."

"Do your parents own the house?" asked the man.

"Of course," said David. "But they don't even know it was there or that we found it."

"Doesn't matter," said the main in a matter-of-fact voice. "I have to talk with them before telling you anything about this map."

The boys stepped away from the counter and started whispering to one another. After a few minutes, they stepped back to the counter and David said, "Okay, I'll call my dad."

"Good," said the man. "And after you reach him, please let me talk to him."

David called his dad and explained that he was with a man who wanted to talk with him about something and then handed the phone over to Mr. Crossbranch.

The man said, "Excuse me" to the boys and then walked into a room at the back and closed the door. After about fifteen minutes he emerged from the room and came over to David.

"Your dad said he would get here as fast as he can. Meanwhile, he suggested that you go over to Amherst

College and look around, like you had planned to, and then come back here. Okay?"

David's heart was pounding as he and Jon left Boston Rare Maps and headed back to his car.

Eleven

Write about someone who is observing their own funeral from out of sight.

Ani

Celebration of Life

I watched the black-clad guests arrive. They filled the seats arranged in a semicircle in the open-air pavilion. I frowned. I had hoped people wouldn't be so sad and subdued. Yet it seemed that every other person was raising a tissue to dab at their eyes, and those who weren't were staring somberly at the wooden floor underlying the pavilion.

The ceremony started promptly at four o'clock, just as I had requested. My husband began by reading several poems selected from Mary Oliver's *Felicity*. I had chosen them to be uplifting, but they seemed to drive more people to tears. The poetry was followed by several close family members sharing stories of my life. I appreciated the sentiment—I really did—but I couldn't help but cringe at being the center of attention. This was supposed to be a celebration of life, and I thought I had made it clear that I hoped that would include all life, not just mine.

The ceremony concluded with one of my favorite songs performed by my son, an up-and-coming guitar player. I had carefully selected a song that was emotional (I didn't want to appear flippant) but who was also intended to produce an uplifting and hopeful tone. It was meant to be a song that would inspire people to feel all the paradoxes of life—the joy in sadness, the hope in loss. To my chagrin there were just more tears.

Finally the ceremony ended. Now was the time to celebrate! I had requested the ceremony to end promptly at five thirty so the guests could leave the pavilion and enjoy the evening light cast by the setting sun. There were lawn games and board games set up, my hope being that people would celebrate my love of games by indulging in play. For the meal I had requested pizza—none of those dainty finger foods they served at traditional funerals that never filled you up—and strawberry pie for dessert.

As the pizza was served, I settled back, watching as people nibbled at slices of wood-fired pizza and gingerly took up positions at tables laid with chess boards, backgammon, decks of cards, dice. I wished that the vivaciousness of the younger attendees would rub off on the older generations. I smiled, watching a boy of about ten (a second cousin's kid maybe?) heatedly debate the efficacy of his opponent's dice roll. That's what I had hoped in planning my funeral—that the event would inspire a new zeal for life! Well, at least the kids seemed to get it.

Someone once told me that "funerals are for the living." Had I been too optimistic in planning a funeral intended to celebrate life? Was it crazy to plan a funeral I would actually *want* to be at? I sighed. This had been it. My last go at influencing the world...gone.

David

Regrets Only

Wow! Three hundred and forty-two people at my own funeral! I read somewhere that the average person knows only fifty-three people well enough that they might attend their funeral. Maybe I'm better than I thought I was. Or maybe they're just angling for money from the foundation I set up! Now's not the time for cynicism, I guess.

Let's see here. There's Dolly, my wife...well, widow... right in the front row. She seems really broken up. That's surprising given the way she often treated me when we were alone together. She was always putting on a show for others. Maybe she's putting on a show now.

There are my sons, Richie and Al. They look fine. They probably are fine, since they now own Shreve & Sons outright. They will no longer have me looking over their shoulders all the time. I remember it was a relief when my dad kicked off, and I took over.

Richie's wife Maddie. Now there was a fox! Too bad we had a family connection or I would have gone for it. Al's wife Linda? Forget it. Mashed potatoes.

There's my accountant Arthur with his dumpy wife Alice. He could be a real pain in the ass, but he sure knew how to cut corners and take advantage of every law and loophole.

Oops, there's my ex-mistress Jennifer, a real sweetheart, sitting only three people away from my ex-mistress Brenda, who proved to be a pain in the ass after I dumped her. Sure hope they don't have a nice cozy chat at the reception.

Over there, in the middle on the right, eight of my fraternity brothers. Those were the days. I sure miss them. They were a riot. And they never bugged me for money.

And then look at all the people from places I gave big bucks to. I'm sure they'll make a big production of introducing themselves to Dolly and my sons. You know, "Oh, Bob, was a wonderful man your father was and so generous." They'll emphasize the word "generous" more than "wonderful," forgetting that they're giving themselves away.

Then there are my neighbors, Ted and Martha. Have to admit they were good people. They didn't get too pissed off when Alfie pooped in their front yard.

Not sure who all those other people are. Seen a lot of them around town. Guess they wanted to see how many came to send off the old man. Oh yes, there's the newspaper editor Frank. He got pissed off when we stopped advertising in his rag. Well, Frank, if no one reads the paper it isn't worth it! And even my plumber Arnie. He had the best jokes!

Looking at all those people makes me wonder what I missed. I wish I could start all over from scratch. With nothing. Maybe I'd have more real friends. Maybe I'd be nicer to Dolly. Maybe I'd become a real wood carver and not just dabble around. Those people selling their stuff at those old country fairs seem happy, even though they're barely making it.

Maybe I'd encourage my sons Richie and Al to do something else with their lives. Richie loves the business, but Al is just going along to get along.

Who the hell knows what I'd do different if I even would? Yeah, I have a lot of regrets, but that's water over the dam. The world will just have to go on without me, and I'll have to go on without the world. *C'est la vie*, as my old French teacher used to say.

Twelve

"She liked to fit people into the world like puzzle pieces."

Ani

Everyday Minutiae

"She likes to fit people into the world like puzzle pieces." That's what they said about me. Not to my face, of course. But I overheard my parents say that to other kids' parents from my hiding place perched on the upper landing of our three-story house. Some iteration of this was usually spoken after a failed playdate when a parent came to pick up whatever kid my parents had tried to have me befriend this time. The line usually came as a grand finale to my mom chattering away about how I was "just quiet" and how no, there was nothing wrong with me, I just "placed a greater emphasis on observation than speaking."

I didn't see what was *wrong* with trying to fit people into the world like puzzle pieces. There was so much to be gained by observing the world around me! Just the other day I found myself fascinated as I watched how a boy in my grade—Carson—held a fork. He stabilized it with his pinky making the rest of his fingers crowd together. *Who had taught him to eat?* I wondered. *Did he hold a pencil the same way?* I incorporated this into my mental image of Carson—"uses fork weirdly."

If someone were to look into my brain, I think they would find some neural equivalent of flashcards for people I've encountered. Some cards would be long with tons of observations printed on them. Others may just contain a word or a short phrase. Carson's card, for example, would contain:

> Reminds me of the color olive green
> Likes talking about himself
> Likes to be in control
> Stressed by uncertainty and disorder
> Uses fork weirdly

Did I know Carson well? Well, no, at least not by conventional definitions of "well." But we'd gone to school together for two years, which was ample time to observe how he engaged with the world.

"Precocious." That was another word my mom used to describe me. Sometimes she called me an "old soul," too. I think these were meant as compliments, although sometimes I wished I didn't remember every little detail I saw in the world, wished I could let go of observing everything all the time. It wasn't that I *tried* to notice the world around me. It was impossible not to! And I wasn't under any delusion that there was some puzzle of the world that I was trying to solve, but life was certainly more interesting when you noticed the minutiae of the everyday, observed individuals' quirks and idiosyncrasies. And talking often got in the way of the simple act of paying attention to the world and people around you.

But I guess that was my problem and why I had so many failed playdates.

David

Just Desserts

Miss Madeline Moggle had a reputation. Everyone who was anyone in New York City knew that Miss Moggle gave the most fabulous monthly dinner parties in the city at her spacious penthouse suite on Fifth Avenue. Exquisite food cooked to perfection by the city's top chefs. The very best French wines. Sometimes she brought in famous opera singers like Maria Callas to sing their favorite arias. Sometimes popular singers like Rudy Vallee. She had Frank Sinatra once, when he was just starting out. Miss Moggle always wore her favorite party outfit: a scarlet velvet gown (size 20) with a gardenia and, of course, her pearl necklace and pearl earrings. She would put a special diamond collar on her miniature poodle Alfie for the occasion.

While enjoying the very best food and wine and music, the guests would always be asked a piercing question by Miss Moggle. Sometimes it was spiritual: "Do you believe in the afterlife?" Sometimes it was a bit racy: "When did you first go to bed with someone?" Nobody dared not answer. That was the price one paid for admission. And then the eight guests—always four women and four men—and Miss Moggle would retire to the massive living room to drink brandy, smoke cigarettes (or cigars for the men), and play parlor games like whist or backgammon or parcheesi.

At eleven o'clock sharp, Miss Moggle would announce that the party was over, and then she would usher everyone out. And the eight guests would go home all atwitter, eager to tell everyone about the party—what was served and who performed music and what the piercing question was. And they would breathlessly await the report in the gossip columns about who was seen entering—or leaving—Miss Moggle's apartment.

After many, many years of maintaining this marvelous tradition, Miss Moggle started getting bored. And tired. At the age of eighty-two, she needed to do something to liven up things, to get her juices flowing again. She also knew she couldn't go on like this much longer. So she came up with a plan. She let it be known to all the gossip columnists in the city that she would sponsor a competition. She would host her dinner parties in the traditional manner for the next eight months. Then she would select one person from each of the eight parties to attend a special Final Party, her last hurrah. It would be held two weeks after the eighth party. Each guest would receive a big monetary award for advancing to the finals. And there would be a special surprise at the end of the evening.

The announcement caused a great commotion all around the city. Everyone wanted to be invited, of course; everyone was determined to reach the finals and get the monetary prize. Everyone wondered how much money would be given; and everyone wondered what the final "surprise" might be.

Miss Moggle spent long hours selecting the eight finalists. She wanted the perfect blend. It was like putting together a puzzle; everyone had to fit in just right. At last she decided on the list. Then she sent out the invitations using a special form of delivery: a team of horses which, on most nights, gave romantic rides for young couples around Central Park.

(Eight months and two weeks later.) The big day for the Final Party arrived at last. Miss Moggle put on her customary dinner party outfit; then she added an extra splash of her favorite French perfume (Parfum du Belle Mort) for good measure. Her heart fluttered rapidly in anticipation. This was her final exam, her ultimate test, her masterpiece, the coup de grace.

The chefs—one of whom was flown in from the Epicure in Paris, a Michelin 3-star winner—were told to prepare their favorite lifetime recipes, sparing no expense. Extra bottles of the best wines were ordered. Marian Anderson, the famous African American singer, was invited to attend and perform several duets with Benjamin Gigli from Italy (Enrique Caruso's heir).

When the guests had almost finished their scrumptious meal, Miss Moggle announced that she would skip the customary piercing question and proceed right to the monetary prizes. She handed out envelopes to each person. They looked like fancy wedding invitations, only bigger. Each one was wrapped with a silver ribbon. She said, "You must close your eyes for about ten minutes before you open your envelope. Maurice, my loyal butler, will ring a bell when it's time to open your eyes. You can then open your envelopes. When that is done, Maurice will ring the bell again. I will be in the parlor waiting for you."

Everything went according to plan, The guests waited for ten minutes. Maurice rang the bell. The guests opened their eyes. Then there were gasps as, one by one, the guests opened their envelopes. Each one contained a check for a million dollars and a short note that said, "Thank you for adding so much sunshine to my life. You are the best. Love, Miss Moggle."

A few minutes after the last guest had opened her letter and the excitement had died down a little, Maurice rang the bell again. The guests got up and started walking into the living room.

But all was quiet in the living room except for the sound of Enrique Caruso playing on the victrola. One guest looked around, stopped, and pointed over to the far corner of the room. There sat Miss Moggle in a large stuffed chair. Slumped over. Eyes closed. A slight smile on her face. Her dog Alfie was sprawled across her lap. Not moving. Lifeless. There was a small vial with the top removed on the table beside her chair.

"I think you must all leave now," said Maurice softly. "Miss Moggle just wanted to say good-bye. It was the only way she knew how to do so."

Thirteen

Pick a person whom you have encountered in the past year and write a story told from their point of view.

Ani

The Tattooed ER Doc

I walked along briskly despite the intense heat of the sun overhead. It was my day off, but I was still buzzed from work yesterday. It was my first year of residency in the ER. I held my phone to my ear using my shoulder as I marched along. I had called a friend from rehab to tell him about the rush I felt yesterday as we dealt with patients from a particularly nasty traffic accident. I didn't miss alcohol. I know that's what ex-drunks are supposed to say, but it was really true. The five years I had been sober had been a grind of medical school and residency applications. And, weirdly, I got a buzz from long hours in the ER, the thrill of a gnarly trauma patient, the high-stakes nature of working at the intersection of life and death.

It was my days off that were the worst. I still woke up early like I had to for work, drank a French press worth of coffee throughout the morning, and then went for a walk. Walking kept me sane. I needed to be busy. Routines were what had helped me sober up, and days off were the hardest because, inherently, they were supposed to be a break from routine. I tended to spend my days off wandering around the small city in which I lived. I walked loops around neighborhoods, called friends (most of them from rehab), sometimes called my parents although that was complicated. Today I noticed a girl—she looked to be about college aged—watching me from the front porch of a house. Had she heard me talking about the guy who died under my watch yesterday? Her bright green eyes were hard to read, and I didn't want to look for too long. Even though it was only a small liberal arts school in the area, it seemed like college students were everywhere—dominating the coffee shops, walking down main street seemingly oblivious of the people around them. And, of course, I saw my fair share of college students in the ER, usually after a drunken escapade gone wrong. I didn't mind the college students, although I often felt like they acted as if they owned the place even though they only lived here for nine months of the year. Had I been that oblivious in my college days? Probably. College was where my drinking habits had started. What was that girl's story? Had she been out last night? What did her future hold? What did she think of me?

I knew how I came across. I was a big guy, balding, and the tattoos...I had gotten a bunch during my drinking days. Some of them sentimental, most of them a waste of money. I thought about getting them removed, but—I don't know—it felt like they were part of me now, whether I liked it or not. I wish I could wear my scrubs all the time, not just because they covered many of my tattoos, but also because they conveyed an ethos I liked. People generally trusted doctors, respected doctors. It gave me an opportunity to leave my past mistakes behind, to be taken seriously and truly respected.

I finished the call with my friend shortly after passing the girl on the porch. What had she thought of me? Probably had assumed I worked a night job in a bar to support a drinking habit and a predilection for tattoos. Well...I guess she wasn't wrong. That *had* been true at one point, but I liked to think people could change. I believed I had changed.

David

An Ass-Kicking Squashed

Ralph ("Ralphie" to his friends) Walker had had enough. He had had enough of the pussies who claimed to be patriots and Donald Trump supporters, but who never did anything about it except forward emails and posts on Facebook to people just like them. *Why just sing to the choir*, he wondered. *Why not bust up somebody else's choir? Why not kick some ass?*

So Ralphie went out to his workshop in the garage and made a plan. 1) Target the places where lots of liberal wimps get together. He smirked and quickly wrote down: The Farmer's Market, the Unitarian Church, the Health Food Store, Planned Parenthood, and the Toyota dealership. 2) Decide on a plan of attack. Stuff razor blades in food or puncture tires at the dealership? Not bad. Put crosses on the yards of upper middle class neighborhoods and then torch them? Again, not bad, but still too tame. And too obvious, too risky.

And then he got a good idea. I'll drive up and down the main street in town in my pickup truck. And I'll fly three big flags in the back of the truck: an American flag, a Trump flag, and a Confederate flag. And I'll have loud music blasting from the truck, great songs like "God Bless the USA" and "Dixie" and "Take Me Home, Country Roads." That last song is about West Virginia, a big Trump state, a big coal producing state. That'll get those libtards. Seeing me drive up and down the street will piss off those smug bastards.

But then it happened. Three local teenagers had had enough of what became known around town as "the Trump jerk who always drives up and down Maine Street with the Trump flag." So they created their own plan. They would hide behind a parked car with a bunch of water balloons and throw them in the window of the pick-up truck when it drove by. Right at Ralphie's jeering face.

The plan worked to perfection. They got plenty of warning that Ralph was coming because they heard "God Bless the USA" playing from three blocks away. Just as he was approaching, they popped out from behind the car. They all threw balloons toward the window simultaneously. Two of them scored direct hits, right through the window, right at Ralphie's face. Ralphie weren't so durned pleased. The pickup truck screeched to a stop a block away, and Ralphie backed up the pickup truck slowly and stopped right in front of the boys who were cowering behind a parked car.

He got out his shotgun and walked slowly toward the boys, pointing the gun at them. Not a wise move, as it happened. A policeman had chanced to see the boys throw the balloons and he had been walking toward them, just as Ralphie started to point the gun at the boys. The policeman yelled at Ralph, "Drop it and hit the floor."

Startled, Ralphie dropped the gun and lay down on the street. "You're under arrest," barked the policeman, "not just for threatening these boys with your gun but also for disturbing the peace by playing music so loud all the time as you drive down the street."

The policeman put Ralphie in handcuffs and led him away, winking at the boys as he did so. The boys later discovered that the policeman's wife was the chair of the town Democratic Committee.

Ralphie's zany plan had worked for a while, as he really did rile up the town's largely Democratic voters. But justice prevailed in the end, thanks to the ingenuity of three patriotic teenagers.

Fourteen

"Well, what I find very interesting is..." he began, and she sank into her chair, exhaling quietly and turning her attention to the empty fields outside.

Ani

The Peace of Solitude

She stared through the window at the grasses waving in the wind. Coffee had seemed like a good idea. After all, Sophie had suggested she and Nate would "totally hit it off." When Nate had suggested a coffee date at a farm café, she had liked him more. But now that they were here, the butterflies in her stomach were dissipating.

Nate continued chattering on about himself. It wasn't bragging, per se, but it was certainly fueled by some level of ego. Anya knew she wasn't helping. She asked lots of questions, and she didn't volunteer much information about herself...but was it too much to hope for a guy who would notice and engage her? She watched as a particularly strong gust of wind flattened the grass across the field for an instant before it bounced back to lazily swaying in the breeze.

Anya knew she maybe lived in her head too much. When she was a kid, her teachers had always told her parents "she's a watcher." Anya had challenged that notion by proving to be a fiercely competitive Nordic ski racer and an accomplished student. But she also would be first to acknowledge that, while these activities demonstrated a high level of engagement, they didn't necessarily require her to be particularly vocal. Which was exactly to her liking.

When it came to guys, there had only ever been one who she felt really went out of his way to get to know her, to draw her out of her head. And it had felt good. Better than she cared to admit, in fact. But life had taken her and Dan separate ways. Friends had taken to setting her up with potential suitors, none of whom had yet to pan out. And that was fine with Anya. She'd rather be alone than with someone who wasn't perfect for her. But she did miss the feeling of having someone capable of pulling her out of her head, someone who was equally private. Dating Dan had felt a bit like a game—each of them taking turns to draw the other one out. And different elements of themselves had been revealed slowly, over time. It hurt Anya sometimes to know that Dan was still out there.

Nate checked his watch. "Wow, time flies! This has been lovely."

"Likewise."

"We should do this again!" Nate said. "I'd love to hear more about you." Now he asked about her?

Anya smiled and nodded. *What is Dan doing right now?* she wondered, as she gave the waving grass one last look on their way out.

David

Putting it on the Table

"Well, what I find interesting is that Fred Thompson, the best man at our wedding, said to watch out for you, that you would do your own thing, that you might have affairs, and that you would leave me some day. I didn't want to hear that warning then, but Fred was right." Mitch Banford, spoke in a monotone, sad, raw, resigned.

Mitch and Samantha ("Sam") had had many such discussions over the years about "the state of our marriage," but he'd never been this honest, never confessed that he'd been warned about the outcome right from the start. It was as if they had been together in a boat that had capsized in a violent storm, and now they were clinging to the floating debris, drifting slowly apart.

"Well, I was warned too," began Sam, after taking a few deep breaths. "My sister said you were wrong for me, that you were too rigid, too controlling, too by-the-book. I didn't want to listen either."

"So," Mitch said, his voice rising above the monotone, "Is it 'by-the-book' to believe that people in a marriage should be faithful? And whatever happened to that 'love, honor, and obey' stuff when we got married?"

"If you want to get all religious on me," retorted Sam, turning up the heat, "what about your promise to 'love, cherish, and honor' me? Is it loving me never to allow discussions of our real feelings? Is it cherishing me to spend all your time watching television or playing games on your phone? Is it honoring me never letting me know the real state of our finances?"

Silence on both sides. Mitch and Sam knew, from past experience, that nothing good would come from this confrontation.

"Let's look on the positive side," pleaded Sam quietly, seeking a détente. "What has been positive about our marriage, such as it is?"

Long pause. "Well, we have three great sons," admitted Mitch, "none of whom got too screwed up by living in our house."

"They sure learned how not to treat a woman in marriage," said Sam, unable to resist the gibe.

Rather than take the bait, Mitch paused and slowly sipped his scotch. "Well, we've both made mistakes," he admitted, with a shrug. "No one's perfect."

"You're not perfect?" Sam laughed, "That's the first time you've ever admitted that! Thank you. I wish I'd recorded that."

"Well, I'm just a new age man," said Mitch, "all sensitive and touchy-feely. What do they call it, 'woke'? I'm woke. That's me! 'Woke Mitch.'"

Sam couldn't help laughing. It was the first time she'd laughed with her husband, not at him, in months, maybe years.

A long silence. They looked directly at each other. Sam thought she saw tears forming in Mitch's eyes. Maybe it was the scotch. Or not.

"Let's go to bed, Mitch," said Sam, "maybe we can talk again tomorrow about where we go from here."

"Yeah," agreed Mitch. "Let's go to bed."

Fifteen

Everyone is born knowing the day they are going to die.
Write about a character whose day of death has already
passed, but they are not dead.

Ani

An End-of-Life Fault

M y heart raced as I woke up on November 14. I was
still here. Was that a good thing? I guess...but I
couldn't really be sure.

I remember analyzing a Shakespeare quote in my
senior English class: "The fault, dear Brutus is not in
our stars, / But in ourselves, that we are underlings." It
doesn't get more cliché than that in a senior English
class, right? Anyway, seventeen-year-old me inter-
preted the quote as Cassius telling Brutus that it's not
fate that makes humans fallible, but rather our own
failings. This may have been true in Shakespeare's
world, but it seemed silly when my classmates and I all
knew what day we were going to die.

Fifty years ago there was a scientific breakthrough
that allowed scientists—specifically biogerontolo-
gists—to assign death dates. A little line—"Expected
death date"—had been added under the "In Witness
Whereof" statement on birth certificates now. My
expected death date was November 12, 2213. Two days
ago, now. I was, still am...I guess, thirty-three.

Let me tell you that living while expecting to die
at thirty-three has not been easy. College felt like a
waste—I'd barely have time to start a fulfilling career,

so what was the point? And starting a family seemed rash when I presumably would abandon my nonexistent wife early and never live long enough to see my kids grow up. So I had kept to myself for most of my life. Getting attached to anyone or any place felt too hard. I had gone to college, which seemed like an ideal way to have a community with a set end date. And I had discovered that I was actually a decent writer. I'd lived in New Mexico for several years in a small adobe house with a peach tree outside, working for the outdoor program of a local private school and as a freelance writer. I had met a girl there—Sara—she had been lovely, perfect in fact, but it got complicated. One night, after I had, once again, expressed my fear that this was getting too serious, she had asked me, "Are you cursed?" I didn't know what to say. I didn't know that many other people's death dates. It wasn't something people talked about. So I didn't know if dying at thirty-three was lucky or unlucky, but I did know that it felt too young to me and I had decided the best thing to do would be to live my life in relative solitude. I knew I had hurt Sara. I hurt, too. If I had wanted a person in my life I was pretty certain it would have been Sara. But that was unfair to her, so I left New Mexico.

Since then, I'd been holed up in Belgrade, Maine. I lived on Great Pond and loved starting and ending my days on the lake. I relished kayaking around the various islands, hiking on the nearby Kennebec Highlands trails, the seasonal departure of tourists that left the lake in a state of utter calm...It was here that I had hoped to wait out my days: writing, woodworking, reading Stephen King's entire oeuvre.

Two days ago, on the morning of November 12, 2213, I had woken up early. Whatever life-force drove us all forward had brought me to a rustic cabin in the backwoods of Maine, so I figured my death would either be a freak accident in the house or a peaceful drift into the abyss while I slept. I drank my coffee while listening to the water lap the shores of the lake, and then I had a normal day. I read (Stephen King's *The Institute*), worked on my current wood project (a jigsaw-cut outline of a sun that I envisioned hanging in a kitchen window someday), and wrote a short story (the last I would ever write, I thought) But the day had passed, and I had gone to bed and woken up on November 13th. And now again on November 14th.

Had there been a fault in the system of predicting death dates on the day I was born?

I was sitting by the lake, gripping my cup of coffee tightly with both hands in an attempt to ward off the chill wind blowing off the lake. I didn't know how to move forward. My life was supposed to end at thirty-three and I had *always* known that. Now I didn't know if I would die tomorrow or in sixty years. The future was uncertain...it could be anything. I didn't know whether to laugh at this ambiguousness or just kill myself now to take away the uncertainty.

Eventually, long after the dregs of coffee had turned cold in my cup, I made my way back up to the house, picked up the phone, and called Sara.

David

Death Interrupted

Al had done what needed to be done to prepare for his preordained death on November 13, 2042. He'd paid all his debts, finalized his will, said good-bye to his friends and family, and made peace with his God, even though he wasn't the overly religious type. Why worry about whether he was going to heaven or hell, since that issue had probably been predetermined as well. He had tried to be a good person because all of his family members were good people. They seldom strayed outside the lines, being nice Midwesterners and all.

Every person knew the date they were going to die, so they were prepared for the occasion as were their friends and family members. The family had given Al their final blessings, and headed off for The Gathering Place in the mountains, which was where families would spend a week to reflect on the loss of their loved one.

For Al, it was now just a matter of lying down for a few hours until he stopped breathing. And then the Final Squad would come and take his body away. He lay down on his bed at eight in the evening; the Final Squad was due to arrive at ten. But then it happened. Or, rather, it didn't happen. Al didn't die. And the Final Squad never came.

Al sat up and looked at the clock beside his bed, which read 10:30 p.m. What should he do now? There were rumors that a few people in the world every year didn't die on their appointed date. No one knew why. Maybe it was just a freak of nature, like being born with three feet or one eye. He didn't know what those people did after they got a reprieve, because it was very rare and very hush-hush. And he didn't know whether they got assigned a new death date.

Al jumped out of bed to call his wife Marge who, he knew, would be surprised and, he hoped, thrilled that he didn't actually die. But then he had a second thought. Why not go somewhere else and start a new life? He still maintained a youthful appearance at age sixty-eight. The ladies still found him attractive. He could still drop down and do twenty pushups without breaking a sweat. Marge was destined to die in two months anyway. His two kids were all set and off living their own lives. After all, he reasoned, who among us has not dreamed of starting anew at some point?

Then the solution hit him. The Villages, that planned retirement community in Florida where the women outnumbered the men three to one. They had lots of golf courses in The Villages as well as restaurants and bars and bridge games. They were mostly Republican, but he could learn to live with that. Or maybe he would even become a Republican, just to see what it was like. The sky's the limit. He could do what he wanted and make up for his lost youth. Al and Marge had gotten married right out of high school, so he had had no opportunity to play the field before settling down. Now was his big chance.

So that's it. He'd go down to The Villages. No one there would need to know that he was one of the rare lucky souls who survived the designated death date. He'd call his trusty lawyer Marty who would have no compunction about changing Al's will and arranging to have a million dollars wired to him to start a new life. So he called Marty's cell phone and left an urgent message: "Hey, Marty. Call me right away! I need a favor. I need you to wire me some money."

Then he went into the bathroom, trembling with excitement and anticipation. Just think about it: he had prepared himself mentally to die, and instead of dying he was going to a nice warm retirement community to spend whatever time he had left living the life of a playboy, a far cry from the life of a nerdy accountant. He spent almost an hour in the bathroom, planning his escape, deciding upon a new name and creating a fake story to tell the people at The Villages. He felt giddy when he came out of the bathroom.

His cell phone was on the bed. There was a voice message on the phone. It was from Marty. Shaking, he listened to the message, "Hey, Art, it's Marty. You didn't answer your phone so I called Marge to tell her I had gotten an urgent message from you, something about sending you some money and asking her what was up. She was in complete shock. She hung up on me. Call her before you call me back. Bye."

Sixteen

Someone does something extreme to return a borrowed item from many years ago.

Ani

The Kept Book

I hadn't talked to Isla in three years.

I generally knew what was happening in her life through the glimpses provided by social media. Following our senior year of college, she moved to Utah to spend a winter season working as a ski patroller before starting a master's program in glaciology at some Scandinavian university. Now she was living in Nepal for a year researching rates of glacial melt in the high Himalayas. At the same time I was working with a nonprofit in Switzerland to develop country-wide guidelines for regenerative agriculture. I brought the book with me to Europe. Its blue-green cover was fading, and almost every page now wore the marks of having been dog-eared at some point. Isla had lent it to me during our senior spring, and it had been (maybe still is?) her favorite book.

I, of course, had read it immediately but, in the whirlwind of senior spring, had never returned it. Isla was a complicated figure in my life. She knew me well—probably better than most people in my life, even to this day. We had been more than friends at one point, but, both ambitious, we felt like we were destined to be pulled apart in the years after college so had kept it casual. I had dated some in the years since college, but had been moving around enough that a stable, long-term relationship had never really seemed possible. And, if I'm honest, I still thought about Isla. It was probably silly, I know. I mean, we had never really dated, so I had no reason to think it would actually work out. But being with her had always felt so easy and effortless. I had always thought that we should give us a real try, but the timing had never worked out.

When I decided to move to Europe for this job following two years of a master's program in environmental management at the Yale School of Forestry, I had found *Sophie's World* amid a stack of books in my apartment. I opened the cover to where "Isla Anderson" was written. It would have been easy to just get rid of the book then—I was packing light for Switzerland—but somehow I couldn't bring myself to leave her favorite book, so I brought it with me.

One evening, while walking by the shores of Lake Brienz in the town of Interlaken where I was living, I thought of Isla. The startling blue of the lake reminded me of the shade of blue on the cover of *Sophie's World*. I took out my phone—but it was late in Nepal, and Isla probably wouldn't be up. I didn't even know if her number was the same as it had been in college.

Over the next several days, I found that I couldn't get the idea of talking to Isla out of my head. Sure, maybe we wouldn't have much to talk about, but I also felt like we had everything to talk about. The past three years had been full and adventurous for both of us, and there was so much ground to cover. If we could just pick up where we had left off as friends...

A week later and I was Googling flights from Switzerland to Nepal. I hadn't used any vacation days this year and had always wanted to go to the Himalayas, so I booked a ticket. Maybe I was crazy, but I figured the worst that could happen was that I had a solo vacation in the mountains.

The day before leaving, I logged onto Facebook and started a new chat to "Isla Anderson":

Hey, Isla, hope you're doing well! I'm going to be in Kathmandu this coming week and would love to catch up. I know this is probably long forgotten, but I have your copy of Sophie's World *to return. I'll bring it with me. Hope to see you soon!*

David

A Lost Life Found

I was cleaning out my office, the long-postponed purge of stuff that I will never need and my sons will never want. And then at the bottom of a big cardboard box in the far corner, I found something that gave me pause—and heartache. It was the beer-stained diary of my freshman college roommate from fifty years ago.

How did I get his diary and why did I still have it? Good questions. My roommate, Peter Payton, was a sad and sorry case. He came from a wealthy family in Seattle who had shipped him off to boarding schools in the East when he was only twelve years old. His parents paid him little attention, even when he returned home for Christmas vacation and the summer. And his only sibling, a sister, was twelve years younger.

Peter had no friends in college. He never studied. I think he was smart, especially in math, but I didn't really know. He never dated; he might have been gay, but no one came out back then. Many nights he'd sit on the couch in our room and drink until he passed out. Usually vodka, but sometimes bourbon. We never talked much. He had little to say. And, to be honest, I didn't want to spend much time with him. I was busy studying and making friends and working for the college newspaper. I didn't want to get weighed down by his problems.

One night in mid-November, out of brazen curiosity, I started rummaging through Peter's desk and found his diary in the bottom drawer. I took it—I can't believe I did that—and hid it in the bottom drawer of my desk, planning to read it over Thanksgiving vacation.

The next day—yes the very next day—Peter disappeared. Boom. Gone. No forewarning at all. This was in 1969, the time of the Vietnam War, and students were worried about the draft lottery number they were going to get. Maybe he got a low number. Whatever. He just vanished. Kaput. Gonzo.

When he didn't show up for classes, his professors notified the dean of academic affairs who, in turn, contacted the dean of students. The dean of students called and grilled me about Peter's whereabouts, but I knew nothing. I guess someone called his parents, but I heard nothing more about it. He just kind of vanished.

I spent the rest of my first year with another student whose roommate had left. He was a good, uncomplicated guy, and that worked out well. I basically forgot about Peter, and I guess I put Peter's diary with my stuff when I moved out after my first year.

Every few years I wondered about what happened to Peter Payton, but I didn't really think about him until the day I found his diary.

So I decided to do some research with the intention of returning his diary to him or someone in his family. Thanks to the wonders of the internet, I found a clue to the whereabouts of my missing roommate. It was his obituary, which had run in the *Seattle Times* in 2012. Peter had fled to Canada, like many other young men trying to evade the draft. He had gone to some college up there and gotten a degree in math. After working as a bookkeeper for several years, he switched to the computer field, right when it was beginning to take off. The obituary described him as "a loner devoted only to his job and the opera. According to his landlord, Peter sometimes read the Encyclopedia Britannica "just for the fun of it." The obituary listed the name of Peter's only surviving relative, a sister, Francine Oberville, a retired history teacher from Seattle.

After some more research, I found Francine's phone number. When I called, no one answered, so I left a message saying that I was Peter's first year college roommate, and that I had something very personal of Peter's that she might want. I asked her to call me so I could return it to her.

That night Francine called me at home. She sounded quite old, even though she would only have been in her mid-sixties, by my reckoning. I explained that I had just found Peter's diary. She seemed both shocked and touched, I sensed that she was trying to hold back tears. She said that I could send it back through the mail.

I told her that I wanted to fly out to Seattle to meet her and give the diary to her in person. That was the least I could do to honor the memory of her brother, my lost roommate. She seemed happy about that.

Seventeen

A woman obsessed with thriller novels wonders if the new man in her life is secretly a top-level government spy.

Ani

My Romantic Story of Dating a Spy

I lay in my bed staring at the small glowing light on the smoke detector on my ceiling. Why was his apartment so sterile? Where were the pictures of family? Friends? The cheesy mugs that almost every-one had some version of? I rolled over onto my side. I was being silly. Dan was probably just a neat freak. And I had only known him for a couple weeks, so it wasn't weird that I hadn't heard much about his past, right? Maybe he was just a really private person? But yet, he was upfront about other things—like that he spoke four languages, including Russian, and had clearly traveled extensively. Why would he tell me that but not give me any background on where he had studied or whether he had a family? Did he have something to hide? And he was in such good shape for someone who claimed he had no athletic interests. Why? My heart started beating faster. He was totally a spy! I didn't know whether to feel excited or scared. It took me a while to fall asleep after this revelation. But I finally did, my last gaze before closing my eyes for good resting on the shelf of thriller novels lining the shelves by my bed.

David

Too Good to Be True

Susan Miller was a sucker for thrillers. When she was a young girl, her Aunt Mabel introduced her to the addictive spells of Agatha Christie and Arthur Conan Doyle. As a teenager, when other girls were having crushes on "that cute boy in (fill in the blank) class," she was counting the days until the next Steven King novel hit the shelves. She secretly wished that she possessed half the chutzpah of Lisbeth Salander, the fearless protagonist created by Stieg Larsson, the Swedish novelist whose three crime novels became all the rage after his death in 2006.

Susan's fascination with thrillers provided an antidote to her rather humdrum, plain-Jane vanilla life. On lazy summer days when she was feeling somewhat frisky, she would retreat to her room for the latest sexy sizzler by Sandra Brown or Tami Hoag. And she loved luxuriating between the steamy pages of the *Shades of Gray* series by E. L. James. What stimulation could you get from a boy, she sometimes asked herself, that you couldn't get from a book like *Fifty Shades of Gray*?

After she graduated from the State University of New York at Geneseo with fine grades but no clear career prospects, Susan settled for a job as a parale-gal at a New York law firm. She figured that being in

Manhattan would help nudge her out of her comfort zone, a necessary move according to her nagging mother and party-girl older sister Meg.

After living in the city for a few months in the safety of her cocoon, a studio apartment in Greenwich Village, Susan decided she had to do something different, if for no other reason than to get her pesky sister off her back. So she signed up for what she had heard was a "good" dating site, whatever "good" meant. And on the third day on the site she got a "let's meet" ping from a guy who lived just a few blocks away in the Village. After some casual, get-to-know you back-and-forth, which Susan found easy to do because she didn't have to really interact with guy, they agreed to meet at a little Italian place near her apartment. Meg had advised her to do coffee first, not a dinner, so she could gracefully cut the cord if prospects looked dim. Susan decided to ignore that advice. In for a dime, in for a dollar, she reasoned.

When Susan first spotted Marty entering the restaurant, she thought he might be above her pay grade. Curly black hair, deep blue eyes. Brimming with confidence, almost a swagger. But after some idle chit chat, she decided that Marty was really a nice guy, underneath it all. The mellow Camigliano Brunello melted away her anxieties. This guy might just work out well.

And so it did. Susan and Marty's relationship heated up quickly. Walks in Central Park. Movie nights in her apartment. Heated texts back and forth during the day. (Marty worked for a venture capital firm.) Susan got swept away in the throes of her first real love. Marty was smooth, for sure, but he also seemed vulnerable and kind.

But....part of her still felt uneasy when she was home from work, alone in her apartment. Why would

Marty choose her out of all the available women in New York? She saw the way other women stared at Marty when they were at a restaurant or just walking along on the street. But he seemed to like her; he seemed to enjoy the relationship as much as she did.

And there was something else that troubled her about Marty. They'd be in the middle of a good conversation, and he'd check his text messages at inappropriate times. He seemed overly interested in learning about her family, almost like an investigative reporter. And one time when she returned from running an errand, she sensed that he'd been rummaging through her desk, because things on her desktop had been rearranged, and one drawer was slightly open. She was sure of it. And sometimes he'd excuse himself from the table because there was a call he "had to take."

Maybe she was just being overly suspicious. Maybe Marty was stringing along another woman at the same time. But his odd actions seemed darker than that, more mysterious. Susan had read enough thrillers to know when something seemed fishy, strange, not right. So—and she hated herself for it—she installed hidden cameras and recorders around her apartment.

One Saturday afternoon when Marty was at the apartment, Susan told him she had to go out for a couple of hours to do some errands. She hinted that she might bring back a surprise for the night.

The real surprise came the next day after Marty had gone home. The camera showed Marty rifling through all her desk drawers. He took out her address book and began writing down something in his notebook. Even more alarming, he began making calls on his cell phone. The sound recordings picked up bits of the calls. "My contacts...Russia...about to move in...her uncle's involved...this romantic cover up is getting old...."

Susan was in shock. She turned off the recording. She couldn't bear to hear more. How could she have been so naive, so gullible? Things had become clear. Marty was a spy for the government. He was trying to track down her uncle, her mother's brother, the missing family member who had fallen totally off the radar about eight years ago. Her uncle was connected somehow with Russian operatives, and Marty was assigned to find out all he could. Susan had been merely a pawn in the process.

She went into the bathroom bent over the sink and threw up. When she came out she noticed that there was a voice message from Marty and two text messages. She ignored them all.

Eighteen

The flat gray of the morning sky matched her mood. For now, she sat at her desk, her eyes often wandering to the wooden rune stave. Today she would do it.

Ani

The Stave Scandal

The flat gray of the morning sky suggested snow later in the afternoon. Her frown deepened as she sank back into her chair, her eyes wandering to the wooden rune stave laid across one end of her desk.

The past three months had been a whirlwind. Her grandfather had passed away unexpectedly. He had been an archaeology professor at a prestigious university and the aftermath of his passing had involved many public events. What the public didn't know was that, in addition to attending celebrations of life and events honoring her grandfather's life and research, she had been dealing with a trove of artifacts he had collected during fifty years of archaeological digs around the world. Her grandfather's old Victorian house was practically overflowing with artifacts and, as his only living relative, it fell to her to handle his possessions. For three months she had been carefully packaging shards of pottery, arrowheads, and various skeletal remains, and sending them to museums around the world. Of course this also involved lots of time on the phone with museums, figuring out who wanted which items. It was practically a full-time job. It had been enjoyable for a time, but she missed her relatively private lifestyle in the countryside. Her grandfather's passing had plunged her into a spotlight she had never wanted and now...well, now it was about to get even worse.

She finally dragged herself out of her trance and her eyes flicked to the clock on the desk's corner—almost nine o'clock. The National Archaeological Museum in Athens, Greece, would be expecting a call from her soon. A week ago, she had found a long wooden package buried at the back of one of her grandfather's closets. Unwrapping it had revealed a wooden stave carved with runes. It was unassuming, but she had practically dropped it when she realized what it was.

Five years ago, her grandfather had been on a dig in Greece, and there had been a scandal involving a disappearing rune stave that his team had uncovered. There were international headlines for weeks, and her grandfather had returned upset and on edge. She had attributed this to confusion over the loss of a prized artifact. That is, until she had found it last week. She knew reporting her discovery would ruin her grand-father's legacy as a renowned archaeologist. It might may even hurt her own reputation as a Greek scholar. But what else could she do?

She sighed. And reached for the telephone, dialing the National Archaeological Museum.

David

A Time for Reinvention

Stephanie Branson knew it would come, sooner or later. And today was the day. Everything had conspired against her. She had to act, cut ties, reinvent herself. And she would.

She hated her job as a corporate tax lawyer. Why would an idealistic history major want to spend her life helping corporations pay the least taxes possible so that their top executives would get the biggest possible bonuses. Her faculty mentor at Williams College had advised her to spend a few years finding her post-college self before deciding upon a plan. Her practical parents back in Ohio vetoed that idea—not that they really had veto power, but she'd never really cut the cord—and suggested something productive like, say, law school. She acceded to their wishes. Her top grades and excellent LSAT scores helped get her into Duke University Law. And Duke led her to the corporate headquarters of JP Morgan in New York City.

Because Stephanie hated her job, she would numb the pain by drinking. Too much drinking. And because she drank too much, she'd get entangled in inappropriate relationships with men and, at one point, even a woman. She felt like she was on a merry-go-round going round and round to nowhere or, more accurately, a roller coaster heading straight down with no bottom in sight.

She had to quit her job on Monday. She had to stop drinking today. But then what? And then it came to her. Her older brother, Jim. She'd call Jim. That's what.

Stephanie could not have been more different than her brother. Jim was an outlier, a hippie at a time when hippiedom was no longer fashionable; he had never colored between the lines. He dropped out of Reed, a very progressive college in Oregon, after two years because even their loose restrictions were too confining for him. Then he fell right off the face of the earth for a year. Gonzo. Stephanie's parents were devastated, and, no surprise, angry. Jim had always been a difficult child, but nothing as extreme as this had ever happened. Stephanie was only eight years old at that time, so she redoubled her efforts to please her parents. She became, even more than before, the "good" child, the model child.

As it happened, Jim had gone to Alaska where he survived by doing menial jobs: mainly painting houses or landscaping. One year to the day after he left, Jim returned home to Ohio. After his parents had calmed down and forgiven him, mostly, Jim told them of his plans. He would return to Reed, complete his degree and then start an outdoor environment program in the Pacific Northwest for inner-city kids. There was a steely determination to his tone that his parents had never heard before.

"How are you going to pay for that?" asked his always skeptical father.

"Grants and private donations," Jim replied. He didn't share the fact that he'd already lined up some young Microsoft millionaires who seemed eager to put their newfound wealth to a useful purpose. He neither sought nor wanted his father's advice or help.

The program, entitled Northwest Rise, succeeded beyond Jim's wildest imagination, drawing kids from the inner cities along the West Coast and donors from the high-tech meccas of Seattle, San Francisco and San Jose.

Stephanie decided to call Jim the next day, Sunday. It would be an uncomfortable call at first, she thought, because she'd never really forgiven Jim for putting their parents through such grief. Also, it didn't seem fair. She had always played by the rules, and now she was living a miserable life. Jim had always ignored the rules until his Alaskan sabbatical put him back on track. Yet his approach seems to have won.

She had to put sibling resentment aside because she needed Jim's support and advice. So after taking a deep breath, she called, her brother at noon the next day, nine o'clock Pacific Time.

"Jim, it's Steph. I really need your help." There was a long silence at the other end of the line.

" Is it about Mom and Dad?" Jim asked.

"No. It's about me. I'm miserable and I need your help." Another long silence.

"Talk to me," said Jim. And she began....

Afterword

You may wonder, dear reader, about the outcome of the phone conversation between Stephanie Branson and her brother Jim. Well, they talked for two and a half hours. The timing of Stephanie's call proved to be perfect, because Jim was in the process of opening up a new camp in Maine targeted at the same audience (inner-city youth), with a similar mission (change the lives of such young people) and title ("Northeast Rise"). He knew that his sister had the drive and determination to accomplish anything she wanted. And working alongside his sister seemed right somehow, a nice way to begin healing their dysfunctional family. Next step? Call their parents. And then get to work.

Nineteen

Compose a story using these three random words: chandelier, toothache, bolo tie.

Ani

A Surprise Gala

I looked down at my bolo tie...fuck. Would it be better to just not have a tie? I glanced around at the other partygoers—most of the men seemed to be wearing nice silk ties that rested on freshly-starched shirts. Fuck, fuck, fuck.

Julie hadn't mentioned this would be a black-tie gala. And our dates so far had been so casual—a picnic in the park, a hike in the Adirondacks, coffee on the Hudson...I had pegged her as crunchy and lowkey, so when she had invited me to her sister's birthday, I had assumed it would be casual. I stared around—the party was in a massive ballroom with a hanging chandelier. Not casual.

"Hey! You made it!"

I turned to find Julie making her way through a group of people. She looked stunning in a simple blue chiffon dress that seemed to float around her. Her blond hair hung in loose waves around her shoulders.

"Hi, yes, I'm here," I said. "This is so fancy! Is Alison happy with how it turned out?"

Julie rolled her eyes—I knew she often felt her younger sister acted like a princess. "The bar isn't serving the full suite of drinks she requested, and she doesn't like the DJ, but she'll live." I grinned. "Come on, you should meet some of my friends," Julie said, and grabbed my hand, pulling me further into the room.

It turned out that Julie's father was a Wall Street hot shot and her mother the headmistress of a highly-regarded private school in Manhattan. So not only was Julie wealthy, but her parents' work had integrated the family into the New York socialite scene. I found myself in awe of how normal Julie had come across on our first dates—no hint of her wealth and totally unassuming. She was quite a contrast to the flurry of meeting her friends—a mix of tech CEOs, Wall Street gurus, and full-time socialites—who clearly had internalized their social position. I found myself trying to avoid sharing that I was a public high school English teacher.

After an hour of making the rounds I felt exhausted, and it was becoming clear to me that, whether Julie liked it or not, she was of this world. I wasn't sure what that would mean for us; maybe it didn't matter. But I knew I was hitting my limit with this party. How many more times would I have to explain that I was a public school teacher by choice, that, yes, I was aware a bolo tie had been a bold selection, and no, my family was not from New York.

I had had it. I told Julie I had a toothache and needed to leave. I knew it was a weak excuse but I couldn't think of anything better, and really just needed to get away. I glanced back at Julie, standing on the stairs outside the gala venue, as I climbed into a taxi. What would happen with us?

David

Dentist Interruptus

Rudy Sizemore had a toothache. "What a pain in the ass," he growled to himself, although it was really a pain in one of his wisdom teeth, not that he lacked wisdom, at least in his own mind. Rudy's dentist had been bugging him about that tooth for two years, but Rudy was not one to be bugged by anyone. He had made his fortune by calling all the shots, being his own man, running his own small oil company in eastern Oklahoma. If he went to the dentist today, he'd have to cancel his regular Thursday afternoon session with Mitzi, his massage therapist.

Actually, Mitzi wasn't your standard massage therapist; in fact, she wasn't even a massage therapist, although she knew how to use her hands where it counted. Mitzi was the excuse Rudy gave to his wife, Mary Anne, for being "unreachable" every Thursday afternoon. Mitzi was Rudy's mistress. And she would be pissed that Rudy missed another one of their "dates," something that had been happening all too often in her opinion, not that Rudy ever asked for her opinion.

Their arrangement worked well for both of them. Rudy got his needs met for physical and ego gratification. Mitzi got regular gifts from Rudy and thereby convinced herself that she was special, like a society lady who lived in one of those big estates with a fancy-dancy chandelier in the dining room and expensive oriental rugs all over the place.

Mitzi liked the fact that Rudy dressed like a cowboy—cowboy boots, blue jeans, flowered silk shirts and just the "right" bolo tie for every occasion. That said, Mitzi's special occasions with Rudy seldom occurred outside the bedroom of her townhouse. Mitzi had always lived out her life in her own fantasy world, because her reality world was too painful—alcoholic mother, abusive father, limited career prospects for an Oklahoma girl in the 1970s whose best assets tended to fall in the physical realm: big tits, long legs, and blond hair, enhanced by the windswept style that actress Farrah Fawcett wore in *Charlie's Angels* and that hordes of the nation's teen girls copied back then.

Finally, Rudy made his decision. He'd go to the dentist and get that tooth taken care of once and for all. Mitzi would have to wait for next Thursday. She'd still be there and the toothache would be gone. Rudy smiled to himself, and twirled his tie. He sure knew how to live. He was the luckiest guy in the world.

Twenty

The floor tasted like....

Ani

Growing Pains

I grimaced as I bent my head toward the gray linoleum floor. I couldn't believe I was doing this. I didn't have to, right? I mean, dares weren't binding or contractual. We were just being stupid kids. But I knew the shame I would face if I refused a dare. It's funny, I thought. I spent hours convincing my parents I was old enough to not have a curfew, old enough to decide to have cereal for every meal if I wanted, old enough to have a girlfriend—or at least to want one, old enough to decide what I wanted for myself in life. And yet, here I was, not able to tell my friends I was old enough to ignore a dare.

I placed my hands on either side of my head, now close enough to the floor to see the texture of different dirt particles and crumbs of food that littered the floor and the faint gray lines of the tile pattern. I heard my friends sniggering behind me.

"Ten seconds," Jake said, as if I could have forgotten. Ugh. I stuck out my tongue and started scraping across the floor. I could detect faint changes in microtopography between tiles with my tongue, and the floor was cold and oddly dry. I don't know if I could have pinpointed a taste. Dirt maybe? Ten seconds felt like eternity.

When I finally got up, my mouth was dry and I resisted the urge to spit; the dare had explicitly demanded a swallow at the end of the licking the floor. Ugh ugh ugh. My friends seemed oddly disappointed I had done it. Well, I guess I could at least feel some pride at surprising them.

"Hey guys, I've got to run, I've got curfew." As I walked home I realized I'd never felt so grateful to have a curfew in my life. Maybe at fourteen I wasn't ready to be an adult yet.

David

A Taste for Detective Work

The floor tasted like stale beer...and dried vomit... and, gross, leftover pizza. Braxton Johansson feared he'd made a mistake when he let his daughter have a "little party with just two friends" in the swimming pool outside their home in Charlotte, North Carolina. His daughter Melinda ("Mellie" to her friends and family) had called him while he was away on a business trip in San Francisco, wrapping up a sweet deal to sell his company. He was feeling generous. What the hell. He could trust her. After all, Mellie was "daddy's little girl." She wouldn't lie about it, would she? What's the worst that could happen? And her mother— Braxton's ex-wife—lived just a few miles away if any problems occurred.

Well, the "the worst" did happen. When Braxton got home around midnight on Saturday night, he noticed the fetid smell in the kitchen. That's when he decided to get down on his knees and smell the floor. And that foul smell prompted him to review the video from the security cameras placed strategically all around the house.

"Jesus Christ!" The "little party with just two friends in the swimming pool" proved to be a big beer blast with thirty-five rowdy teenagers ransacking the house.

They had jumped up and down on the new pool table. And banged on the piano he'd bought for his two kids to give them some culture. And played a drinking game while sitting sprawled on the living room floor. Where the hell did they learn that game, he wondered, before remembering that kids in this affluent community had older siblings who'd learned all about drinking games—and Lord knows what else—in college.

They had tried to clean up the place a bit, he deduced, as nothing had seemed immediately out of place when he first walked in. But their cleaning repertoire did not include a recommendation for "cleaning floors that have been splashed with beer and pizza."

Braxton decided he'd clean up the mess the next day. Or, rather, he'd have Mellie and her friends clean it up while he "supervised." And then he'd talk with his ex-wife to decide upon the right punishment for this flagrant violation of their trust.

He decided to sleep late the next morning because he was exhausted from his trip to San Francisco, and he was not looking forward to confronting Mellie. He finally stumbled downstairs at nine thirty on Sunday morning. Just as he hit the bottom stair, he heard the doorbell ringing. He opened the door. It was...Mellie. Her eyes were streaked with tears. She looked lost, defeated, scared, ashamed.

"Daddy, I..." she sobbed, before collapsing in a heap on the floor. "I didn't mean to. Some extra students came by the pool and before we knew it, some other kids started coming over and bringing beer and...."

Braxton looked down on his daughter, his poor little baby girl. In a flash, he recalled some of the wild things he'd done as a kid, most of which he had gotten away with. He remembered the day Mellie was born and how proud he felt and how he would protect her, no matter what happened. His firm resolve melted away.

Slowly, gently, he wrapped his arms around Mellie. He knew how awful she felt about what had happened. She'd already learned a huge lesson. The punishment—he had to level some form of punishment—could come later. "Hey, baby girl," he said softly. "We all make mistakes. We just have to learn from them, right?"

Mellie looked up at her dad with an expression of disbelief and pure love and gratitude. "You're right, Daddy. But I'm so sorry. I want to clean up the rest of the mess."

"I'll help you," said Braxton "Many hands make light work. And when we're done we can take a long walk in the park. I want to hear more about you and what you've been up to. And I have a few stories of my own I'd like to share with you."

"Okay Daddy," she said softly. And gave him a big warm hug.

Twenty-one

Write a story that takes place in an empty landscape.

Ani

Hollow

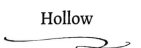

I searched my brain for something, *anything*. I was hoping to find some spark of passion, some big feeling, but...nothing. Facing my nothingness was my greatest fear. I had combatted this fear in high school by obsessively checking boxes—student government president, varsity soccer captain, honors student, valedictorian. I had gone to college burnt out but eager to find a real passion, something that was...well, me. But perhaps I had romanticized college because, after four years, I graduated feeling like I had, once again, performed well but that I still didn't have a passion, a drive, a sense of *my* purpose in the world. I was still just checking boxes.

In the nine years since graduating from Harvard, I had bounced between jobs. A stint at Goldman Sachs followed by a meditation retreat at Christ in the Desert monastery in New Mexico with the goal of re-finding myself after feeling lost in the investment world. I had come out of the meditation retreat with a renewed vigor to find my purpose in life.

I thought my dream was to be a writer, but I didn't know where to begin. In the rearview mirror of life, I know I should have written every day, know I should have pursued writing not as a hobby but as an obsession if that was what I really wanted. But I didn't know how to break away from expectations, from the voices of my parents telling me I needed a "real" job and the knowledge that my friends from college were getting married and settling into careers. So I went back to law school, putting my political science degree to good use, at least in the eyes of my parents. Now I was working at an environmental law firm. I was successful by conventional standards—I made enough money to own a nice thirteenth-floor apartment in downtown Denver; I could afford vacations to Patagonia, Switzerland, British Columbia; I had been dating a woman for two years who was lovely and supportive and smart and beautiful. I had every reason to be happy. And maybe I was *happy* but I was certainly not fulfilled.

So here I was, sitting on the patio of my thirteenth-floor apartment at four in the morning, watching the sky lighten and listening to the sounds of Denver waking up. I had my beat-up, creased journal on the table in front of me. It was open flat and two blank pages stared back at me. When I was younger, I had hoped that at age thirty I would be able to fill pages and pages with stories about my life, adventures I had had, risks I had taken, issues I cared deeply about, and people I cared deeply for. But as I twiddled the pen, searching my brain for something to write about, I found myself at a loss. My mind was an empty landscape.

I sipped my coffee. *You know what?* I thought. *I don't think I'm going to go into the office today.*

David

Giving It Up

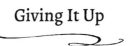

Okay, I'll say it straight: I'd fucked up my life. Drank too much. Cheated too much. Alienated my kids. Pissed off my boss. And, the final straw, got booted out of the house by my wife. Maybe it was time to end it all. Or maybe not. I needed to get away from everything to figure things out. Everything. So I did.

I drove straight from my home in Portland, Oregon, to Death Valley in Eastern California, in the northern Mojave Desert, bordering the Great Basin Desert. It had the right name, "Death," because that's what I thought I was nearing. And "Valley," because I was at the low point in my life. We had studied Death Valley in my college geology class, so I was familiar with some of the essentials: lowest elevation in North America at 282 feet below sea level, extremely hot summers, short mild winters, and little rainfall. It got its name in 1849 during the California Rush after thirteen prospectors died when they sought to cross the valley on their way to the goldfields.

Not every Tom, Dick, or Harry can venture alone into Death Valley without being in great shape and very well prepared. Or if they venture in, they won't venture out. I wasn't worried. I'd spent many of my spare weekends over the last twenty-five years hiking and camping. I knew what was up, and I was prepared.

My plan, in brief, was to drive as far I could into the Death Valley National Park. Then just leave the car and walk as far as I could and then lie down on the desert floor and do some hard-core soul searching. "What fool would take this approach?" you might ask. Well, a fool like me who's always hated the idea of getting raked over the coals by some shrink or attending one of those touchy-feely new age retreats where everyone stripped off their clothes—metaphorically if not literally—and bowed down to some conniving cult leader like a herd of mindless sheep. I didn't need to "process" my thoughts and feelings. I just needed to get the hell away from all the distractions that had led to my disintegration in the first place.

My plan worked to perfection, or at least the technical aspects worked. Exactly one week later, I was lying down on my sleeping bag in the middle of the day on the floor of Death Valley. No one was around for miles. I had toted in enough food and water to last four days. One day walking to my spot; two days there; one day out. That should be enough to figure things out, I thought, and if it wasn't then, what the hell, they could put on my tombstone: "Daniel Forsyth Jones. Challenged Death Valley and Lost. But He Did It His Way."

The first day at Death Valley I just lay on the ground and looked around me and tried to empty myself of all thoughts and feelings. Just got into a zone, kind of like meditating, I guess, but I never got into that stuff. Too sissified for me. It pretty much worked. I felt like a floppy rag doll at the end of the day. And exhausted.

The second day I painted a mental picture in the empty landscape around, treating it like a blank canvas of sorts. I would just stare at this patch of earth or that patch of sky until something emerged right before me, like a mirage. Or maybe a Ouija Board, to get all hocus pocus about it. Basically, I just visualized, looking for signs to follow—people or buildings, some kind of omen whatever. I borrowed a phrase from those Christian wackos who are always saying, "give it up to God," or whoever the hell stands over all of us hapless humans, if anyone does.

Somehow, on that second day, it all made sense. I had never felt at such peace. Never.

On the third day, I started walking back. I say started, because after a few steps I broke into a slow trot. I felt free and easy, like a kid, no worries. After a few hours I got back to my car. Or at least the place my car had been. It wasn't there. Nothing was there. Nothing was around. I was miles and miles away from the exit. But somehow, for some reason, I didn't feel anxious or scared. I didn't panic. Even though my water had run out. And my food was gone. This wasn't a bad way to go.

I sat down on the ground with a smile on my face. Whatever happened happened.

Twenty-two

A woman is standing in her backyard talking animatedly on the phone.

Ani

The Unfinished Game of Chess

I watched my mom's hand go to her mouth and her eyes widen. "Oh my gosh," she said, starting to pace around our yard. I strained my ears. Who was she talking to?

"When did it happen?"

When did what happen? Mom seemed calm, but I noticed her lip trembling as she finished a lap around the yard and started another one. I wanted Dad to come home. We had been waiting on him for dinner. It was my last night before going back to school. I was starting seventh grade, and we were making homemade pizza as my last dinner of the summer. I was kind of excited for a new school, but mostly nervous. Mom and I had been sitting on our patio playing chess while we waited. Mom laughed so hard when I tried to convince her that there was a rule that the white bishops could move in any way they wanted. "You're just saying that because *you're* white," she had teased. Well, true....

"Where are you taking him?" I heard. What was happening? Who was going somewhere. I fiddled with a castle on the chess board in front of me. Maybe we would have time for another game when mom got off the phone.

"Is he going to be okay?" After a pause, I saw Mom's face crumple. "I'm on my way."

Mom hung up and slowly turned from mid-lap to face me. "There was an accident, it's your father, we need to go." As Mom hurried to me, her arms open for a hug, I dropped the white castle onto the board. As I felt her arms envelop me, I heard the castle roll off the board and hit the patio deck behind me.

David

Weighing Secrets

When I looked out the window, I saw my neighbor Sandy standing in her yard, yelling into the phone, or at least it seemed like yelling. Sandy has become a good friend, and it wasn't like her to get so emotional, especially in such a public setting.

After about ten minutes, she got off the phone and went back into her house. I waited about half an hour and then gave her a call to see what was up.

"Hi, Sandy, are you okay?" I asked. "I saw you outside talking on the phone. You seemed really upset. Are you okay?"

"Can I come over, Brenda? I need to talk to someone."

"Sure," I said, and minutes later I led her into the house. We sat down at the kitchen table and talked or, more accurately, she talked, an avalanche of thoughts and feelings that had been dammed up for God knows how long.

"Thank you so much for calling. I had to talk. I'm caught between a rock and hard place or, to be specific, my parents and my husband Tom. They voted for Trump, no surprise because they're part of the Midwestern white Christian evangelical clan. Tom thinks they're stupid or brainwashed or brain-dead. He wants nothing more to do with them because of their religious and political views. I see where he's coming from, but they *are* my parents. I don't want to cut off all ties. My kids—whenever I have them—need to have some connection with their grandparents.

"I had to go outside to call them after the election was called for Biden, because I didn't want Tom to know I was calling them. We tried to listen to each other, but I just don't 'get' their viewpoint. And I guess they don't get mine.

"But that's not the worst part. I wanted to tell them that Tom and I have just been approved to adopt a new baby boy. They've been bugging us about having children for years, but it just hasn't worked out. They should be happy about the adoption news, but there's just one small hitch: the baby is from Haiti. I don't know how to tell them that, so I didn't bring it up during the call about Biden getting elected. Remember, they're from the white Christian evangelical community. They say they're not racist, but you know how it is. That stuff can be subtle.

"What should I do, Brenda? I have to tell them sometime, and I'm afraid of how they'll react."

I took a deep breath and then gave my answer. "Tell them you have a big surprise. You can't tell them what it is, but tell your mother she might begin knitting a blue baby sweater. Don't answer any other questions. Tell her you don't want to spoil the surprise. Tell her that she'll hear more later. She'll be ecstatic. She'll tell all her neighbors and her church friends and she'll begin making the sweater. And probably a baby hat. And mittens. And a blanket. She'll dream about being the grandmother she's always wanted to be. She'll be so invested in the whole idea of a grandson—her first grandchild—that nothing will be able to pop her bubble. Then cross the bridge about Haiti when you get to it. Make sense?"

"Oh, Benda, you're the best friend ever. That's the perfect solution!"

She gave me a big hug and left all happily. I didn't know what else to suggest. I hope my advice proves to be sound.

Twenty-three

Tell a story seen through a window in an apartment in New York City.

Ani

The Bookkeeper's Customer

I watched steam unfurl from my coffee mug as I placed it on the window sill next to an aloe plant and a stack of books that had grown steadily over the past year. The steam from the coffee frosted the glass as I assumed my perch on a rickety wooden chair dragged over from the two-person table so I could sit with my feet resting on the window sill watching the street below.

I lived on the fourth story of a small apartment building in Manhattan. My window overlooked a little side street and offered me a direct view of the comings and goings at The Bookkeeper bookshop across the alley. I loved starting my day with coffee and a glimpse into the lives of book shoppers. Most people didn't stay in for that long; many seemed to enter with a purpose and emerge with a small, paper-wrapped package—a birthday gift maybe? Or perhaps following up on a recent recommendation or a *NY Times* bestseller. Personally, I loved to spend hours browsing bookstore shelves. I liked not having a purpose and just letting myself be open to what books stood out.

On this morning in particular, I watched a man enter. He wore a maroon scarf around his neck to keep out the November cold but his head remained hatless. It was hard to distinguish specific features from my fourth-floor vantage point but based on his style (Blundstones, Patagonia puffy coat, corduroys) I guessed he was cute in an understated way. After I watched him enter, the bell jangling noiselessly on the door as it shut behind him, I sipped my coffee and flipped through the most recent issue of *High Country News*. I had to be one of the only people in New York who subscribed, but I was from New Mexico and considered the West my home, and I was determined to know what was going on in that part of the country. I also loved the large glossy photos depicting landscapes I so often longed for amid the bustle of the city.

I finished my coffee, getting up just long enough to refill my cup and grab my computer from the countertop. I scrolled through Facebook and cleared my email. It had been two years since I had lived with anyone, and then that had really only been a short, summer fling, so maybe it had been longer. I had hoped for more and envisioned much more, but, well, I don't know. I guess Liam had just been in a different place. Since then I had embraced independence with renewed vigor. Liam had made me doubt myself, and my response to that had been to burrow into myself more and just hope that someday someone would be bold enough to come along for the ride.

I loved my mornings spent by the window, drinking coffee, catching up on casual communication. I worked as a freelance writer for *Outside* magazine—we were trying to push the bounds of what it meant to be "outdoorsy," and so here I was, in the middle of New York City, reporting on how outdoor culture converged in one of the world's most populated areas.

As I finished my second cup of coffee I noticed the guy with the scarf leaving The Bookkeeper, a stack of books under his arm. He had been in there for a while. Usually no one stayed in longer than one of my cups of coffee! I was surprised and a little impressed. I caught myself smiling as I turned back to the article I was working on. *If the same guy comes back again, I'll go talk to him*, I promised myself.

The next morning as I set my coffee down next to the aloe plant, I looked out the window. The guy with the scarf and Blundstones was just opening the door to The Bookkeeper....

David

Transfixed

I was beat. A country boy after a long day in the Big Apple. It's a long way between Florence, South Carolina and New York, New York. My day had gone well, and I'd landed a new client, maybe two. But now I was ready to kick back. Have a drink. Even go down to the hotel bar and get into some trouble. Nah, I'm too wiped. One more day in New York City. Don't blow it now.

When I went over to the window to pull down the shade, I happened to look across at the next building, on the floor below. There in the dim light were a man and a woman, just fifty feet away from me. She looked like she was in her early thirties. He was older, maybe forty-five. They didn't seem like a husband and wife, if you know what I mean. Too much tension, sexual tension, I think. Or something else. They were more like...I don't know, a couple about to break up. He looked mad. She looked scared. They'd get close together, right in each other's face, then he'd push her away. Or she'd push him away. Then they'd hug. Almost like a mating dance. But there seemed to be more at stake. You know how a female praying mantis sometimes bites off the head of the male? It didn't look that bad, but pretty intense.

Maybe I should just shut the shade, forget about the couple, and hit the sack. But I couldn't. I was transfixed. Maybe something "good" would happen, a free porno show, a winning lottery ticket! Or not. I felt like a bad little boy peeking in on his parents on a Saturday morning. I began to feel the tension in my own body.

Then, suddenly, I sensed that the tension between that couple was really mounting. He looked angry, menacing. She looked mad too, but hers seemed to be melting away, turning into fear, almost terror. They were standing close together now, like two heavyweight fighters in a clinch. But then slowly, terrifyingly, he put his hands around her neck. Just then, he happened to look out the window. And saw me. Or I think he did. Our eyes locked. I quickly pulled the shade down, my heart pounding. Any budding lust I'd been feeling disappeared just like that, poof, gone.

That's it. The show's over. Have to go to bed, get some sleep. I brushed my teeth, washed my face and crawled into the king-sized bed, feeling like a scared little boy. Heart rate almost down to normal. I lay there for an hour, maybe two. Recreating the last scene of the couple in my mind. Maybe it was nothing. Playacting. Maybe they were into sadomasochism. That's it. She was a paid hooker who specialized in that stuff. But that's too simple. They weren't playacting. Maybe if I could get to sleep, I'd wake up in the morning and barely remember what I'd seen.

But first, one last look. I got out of bed and walked slowly over to the window and looked across to the room on the floor below. The shade was pulled. It was totally dark. Relieved, I began walking slowly back to the bed. I glanced at the clock on the chest beside the bed. 2:13 a.m.

And then, a soft tap on the door, and then more taps, getting a little louder with each tap.

Twenty-four

Other pregnant women craved pickles, fries, and Mexican food. Me? I craved my next door neighbor. He looked me up and down and smiled back, inviting me in.

Ani

Tea on Tuesday

I followed Will into his home. It was a carbon copy of mine right next door, but cozier. There were personal touches like photos on the wall, mismatched throw blankets, books left out. It looked lived in. I couldn't say the same. My husband was a neat freak and so our house was all polished granite countertops, scrubbed white walls, and pressed linens. I put my hands around the bump on my belly. I had no idea what my husband would do when we brought a screaming, dirty, germy child into our perfectly manicured home.

My neighbor Will had become a companion since I'd been stuck at home on maternity leave. He liked to read, and it had started as a friendship built on book exchange, but that had morphed into regular visits for tea or to discuss the news. Will was single and had never been married. My husband and I had been together for two years. Jed and I had met at the end of college and, well, frankly I hadn't seen it going anywhere, but then there had never really seemed a good time to call it off, and he had been willing to change his life to follow me so our lives had melded and now here we were, expecting a baby in three months. Jed was usually gone at work these days. He didn't particularly enjoy working in the financial world, but he'd never tried anything else. I had always prided myself on being an independent, hardworking, determined woman, and it had been painful to leave my job running an environmental nonprofit in rural Maine, but Jed earned more at his job in the suburbs of New York, and we needed that to support the baby.

Will was from Maine—far north in Millinocket. We often daydreamed of the views from Mount Katahdin or the rocky ledges in Acadia National Park. I knew it was wrong, but I could feel myself falling for Will. He was everything I had ever wanted—independent, inquisitive, funny, smart, passionate. Other pregnant women craved pickles, fries, and Mexican food. Me? Well, I craved conversations with Will. He made time slow down, he made me laugh and feel confident in myself. So here I was, just another Tuesday afternoon spent drinking tea with him as we discussed the latest book I had borrowed (*Bucking the Sun*), drank Earl Grey tea, planned the tiny garden we hoped to plant in our shared lawn next spring. It was easy and comfortable. He showed me photo albums from his college days in Colorado, shared writing pieces he was working on, and complained about the difficulties of supporting himself as a freelance writer. He was here in the suburbs of New York to be closer to his mom, who was ailing. He viewed his life here as temporary. I often wondered if he was lonely. At thirty-three, shouldn't he want a partner? Want to start building his life? I think part of me was jealous that he had lived his life as a single individual for so long.

I didn't know how Will felt toward me. I know he didn't have many other friends in our neighborhood and hadn't felt motivated to put in the effort, since he didn't envision being here any longer than he had to.

But I also saw the way he looked at me when I walked in, could sense there were more to his feelings. *Someday I'll ask him about it*, I thought as I said my good-bye and walked across the driveway to our house. The lights were off—Jed was probably going to have another late night in the office.

A few days later I woke up to a text from Will—"I've been assigned a story on dam proposals in Southern Chile. I'm off tomorrow. I'll be out of town for the foreseeable future. xx."

And just like that he was gone from my life.

David

In a Pickle

My heart pounded. I'd been fantasizing about my neighbor Brian for months, I'm embarrassed to say. When he's out in the yard working I find myself taking just a little extra time looking out the window. In fact, a lot of time. He's got the moves. And the muscle. He's a little older than I am, but not so much older that he doesn't know what needs to be done with a woman, if you catch my drift.

A little fantasy never hurt anyone, right? Sure, I've been married for two years, happily so for the most part, and my husband, Hugh, is a good and loyal and faithful man. And we're expecting our first child, which we're both thrilled about. My parents can't talk about anything else, since this will be their first grandchild. I should be happy and content. I shouldn't be thinking about my neighbor doing "those things" to me. Christ, I feel like a hormone-dazed teenager.

Maybe I need to take a cold shower. Or a long run. Or read a nice trashy romance novel to get these thoughts out of my system. Actually, I've tried all those things, and nothing's worked. I still find myself thinking about Brian in the dark of night. Or the middle of the day, for that matter.

Maybe I could just sit down with Hugh and confess that I've been having sexy feelings about our neighbor. He'd understand, right. Hell no, he wouldn't, and I don't blame him, to tell you the truth. Of course, I could think about Brian when I'm being intimate with Hugh, but that's disloyal too, when you really think about it.

Maybe I should just go over to Brian's house and have a cup of coffee with him and apologize to him for what I've been thinking. Yeah, right. That would be like going to the humane society to "just look" at a new puppy that just became available.

Maybe I should just have sex with Brian one time to get it out of my system. Yeah, right. That would be like eating one potato chip.

And then it happened. I went out to get the mail, and there was Brian, watering the flowers, looking like, well, you know....

"Hi, Brian," I said, and the tone of my voice was more than one might call "neighborly." I had tossed the vibe and he had caught it. After all, he's a guy, at least the kind of guy who knows when a woman is interested in him.

"Would you like to come in and have a cup of coffee?" he asked, in a warm friendly tone. We'd had some very casual chats before, but had kept everything aboveboard. Brian and Hugh were friends, and I suspect he didn't want to ruin the friendship. But, again, he's a guy.

I waited a few seconds before answering, my heart pounding. In my mind, I ran through all the possible consequences of "just having coffee" with my neighbor. None of them were good, at least from a long-term point of view.

"Thanks, Brian, but I don't have time today." He smiled, looking a little disappointed.

"Maybe another time though." He smiled again, a different kind of smile.

I went back inside the house.

Twenty-five

A lucky charm is found.

Ani

The Lost Clover

The little girl squatted down in a sea of green and purple. Her legs, scraped and bruised from a summer spent playing outside, folded beneath her as she sank into the field of clover. Her blond hair formed a knotted halo around her face, and she pushed it roughly behind her ears. It was clear from the intensity of her bright green eyes that she was intent on finding something. She combed the field of clover, occasionally using her hands to brush down patches or to pull a stem toward her for a closer look. Anyone watching would have been surprised to see an eight-year-old sitting so still.

After an hour of looking, her eyes lit up and her hand carefully pinched the stalk of a single clover plant, pulling off the four-leaf clover. She cupped it with both hands, grinning as she ran back to the house and up to her room. She scanned her room until her eyes found *Harry Potter and the Goblet of Fire* resting on the bookshelf. She carefully set the clover on her dresser, opened the book to page forty-four—her favorite number—and slipped the clover in between the pages, making sure that it was flat. With that done, she replaced the book on its shelf and skipped downstairs.

Ada proudly told her family about the four leaf-clover she had found that day while they sat outside on their patio eating dinner.

"That's great, honey! I remember finding those all the time when I was your age." her dad said.

"You don't actually think those bring you luck, do you?" asked her thirteen-year-old brother.

Ada's face fell. She should have kept the clover as her secret.

Later that night, after her parents had tucked her into bed, she got up and pulled out *Harry Potter and the Goblet of Fire* off her bookshelf. She had to use two hands to maneuver the thick book off its shelf. She flipped to page forty-four and admired the clover—its four leaves splaying out, the lighter colored lines partway up each leaf...it *was* lucky, she decided as she closed the book and hopped back into bed.

Years passed, and Ada soon forgot about the four-leaf clover tucked away on page forty-four of *Harry Potter and the Goblet of Fire*. She went off to college, leaving most of her books behind. After graduating from college, she was set to move to Switzerland where she would be completing a master's program in glaciology at ETH in Zurich. Her blond hair was longer than it had been when she was eight, but it still often framed her face in a halo of wisps. Ada's green eyes had come to be one of her defining features—garnering her attention from boys throughout college (most of whom she had politely declined) and giving her gaze an intensity that she knew often caught people off guard.

Ada pulled back her hair as she faced her new apartment in Zurich. She hadn't brought much but she had brought her *Harry Potter* collection, and, as she was neatly ordering the books on the shelf next to her bed, she saw a flash of color whirl.

Ada smiled, her green eyes lightening with happiness as she stared at the four-leaf clover resting on the floor.

David

In the Clover

As I was walking from the condo to my Hyundai, I chanced to look down for no good reason other than the fact that I was feeling depressed. And there it was, in a small patch of grass next to the driveway: a four-leaf clover. Not only that, there was another four-leaf clover just six inches away. A double dose of good luck in one fell swoop.

What on earth did I do to deserve a double good luck charm? Not that I couldn't use a break, God knows. My girlfriend had just broken up with me, totally without warning or a good reason, at least as I saw it. Something about my "unwillingness to make a commitment." You know, the go-to line for women in their early thirties who've come to the "shit or get off the pot" moment. There's a reason that women who use lines like that can't catch a man, but what the hell, there are more fish in the sea, as my wise college roommate Bennie used to say. He had other lines like, "If you miss the first bus, just wait; there will be another one along in just fifteen minutes. Real philosopher, that Bennie.

Not only that, my boss had reamed me out in front of my peers last week, not something he had learned in business school management 101 in, I daresay. But, whatever.

So here I am. Forty-one years old. No girlfriend. Job on the rocks. I'd quit the job if I had something decent lined up. As to finding a new girlfriend, I sure don't want to have to go through all that dating site crap again. Too inefficient.

Well, I have to do something to get out of this funk. Maybe the four-leaf clovers will lead me to something, something good, like a divining rod helps you find water. Bennie would say that he had a "divine rod," but whatever. Enough about Bennie. So I went down to Smiley's that afternoon, the Irish bar in the South End where people like me tend to go to knock down a few and maybe get lucky. Young women like to go there because it's fairly safe as those things go.

I'm sitting at the bar at Smiley's drinking an Amstel Lite, when I'm not crying in it, and a cute young woman sat down beside me. Well, she wasn't that young. In fact, she was probably about my age. And she wasn't that cute, but she'd pass for now, for sure. An eight on a scale of ten. Let's just say that Bennie would have approved.

Feeling brazen after two beers, I took one of the four-leaf clovers out of the handkerchief in my pocket and shoved it across the bar to the woman. "Ever find two of these at one time?" I asked in my suavest manner.

She looked down at the clover and then up at me. When she did, I could see that she had been crying. Either that or she had a bad cold. Maybe hay fever.

"No, I haven't," she said in a voice just above a whisper. "Have you?"

"Yes, I did this very morning," I said, trying to sound kind, not boastful. I could see that this was a sensitive woman, not some chick on the move. "It came at a good time, because I've been down on my luck. Since I found two four-leaf clovers, I decided to give you one of them. You know what they say, 'Pass it on.'"

She smiled and I could sense the tension leave her body. "Why are you down on your luck, if I may ask."

"You may," I said, and gave her a quick recap of the unfortunate turn of events that brought me to this bar on this day. "But what about you? How's your luck going?"

"I've been better," she said, and slowly spun out her own tale of woe. Got divorced two months ago. No kids, although she'd always wanted kids. "I'm feeling down. No good reason. My job at the Museum of Art is going well. My health is good. But something's missing."

She looked right into my eyes when she said, "Something's missing." I knew right at that moment that we had to keep this conversation going. We had to take it up to the next level, as sports announcers always say. And we did. For two and a half hours.

We traded life stories, as much as you can in a setting like that, and then traded phone numbers. I knew I wanted to see her again, and I sensed that she felt the same way. I had a wise old teacher once, who used to talk about the "spirits of the universe." Well, the spirits were with me and Anna Jenkins—that was her name—that day.

Just as we were getting up to leave the bar and part ways (for now), I got a text from my friend Joey at work. "Guess what, dude? The asshole quit!" By "asshole" he meant our mutual boss Barry. "Seriously?" I texted. "Yea," replied Joey, Let's go grab a few beers and celebrate!"

I let Joey know that I couldn't get together that night, but that we'd do so real soon.

"Hey, Anna," I said, turning to my new friend. "Those clovers and this day have brought me more luck that I could ever have imagined. Can we get together for dinner some night?

"Why wait? How about tonight?" She said, without skipping a beat. I liked her. Warm, direct, to the point. "Sure." I said, and we headed down the street to find the right dining spot for our first date.

Twenty-six

It was a hell of a way to die.

Into the White Abyss

They had backcountry skied into the cabin the night before. Nestled at the base of towering mountains in the Alps, it was the perfect getaway for Grace and Jack. They'd only been dating for a year, but it had been a whirlwind—Jack had finished earning his MBA, and he and Grace had decided to get an apartment in New Haven together while Grace completed the last year of her master's in environmental management at the Yale School of Forestry. Life was moving quickly. For Christmas they had decided to skip all the family stuff and just go to the mountains together.

Their first night at the cabin had been exactly what they hoped for. The small wood stove cranked out heat to such a degree that they had both stripped down to their lightest layers. They had happily made pasta with sautéed mushrooms, foregoing their camp stove to cook over the heat of the fire. And they had ended the night snuggled together on the small, bottom bunk of the cabin reading from Mary Oliver's *Felicity*.

They woke up to fresh snow. A light powder piled up on the window ledges and Grace had to work to force the door open against the weight of snow that had accumulated during the night. They flipped pancakes in a skillet balanced atop the wood stove while they sipped their coffee and slowly put on layers for a day outside. They were hoping to ski partway up the peak directly behind the cabin and cruise down in the fresh powder.

As they fastened their skins to the base of their skis outside the cabin and set off, Jack heard a rumbling in the distance. He glanced around, but the snow conditions seemed okay. He and Grace weren't that concerned about avalanches today. They kept going, occasionally glancing back to see the cabin looking smaller and smaller behind them.

For lunch they stopped, dug a little ledge in the snow, and perched there to eat peanut butter sandwiches that had smooshed in their pockets during the morning ascent. As they turned their faces to the sun, there was a distinct rumbling. They turned simultaneously to see a wall of snow from high up on the mountain begin to slide, picking up speed as it headed toward them.

Jack's wild eyes found Grace's. He thought of the life he had envisioned for them—a little home, kids, definitely a sun porch, maybe some chickens and sheep, more vacations spent in the mountains. And he thought of the serendipitous choices that had brought him to this moment—growing up in a small town in Vermont where skiing was just what everyone did, falling in love with the mountains as an escape from the bustle of life, meeting Grace while hiking in the White Mountains....

Grace's mind flashed to her family at home in Maine—what were they doing right now? She thought of her apartment in New Haven, how she had never told Jack that she loved sharing it with him, that she wanted to build a home with him. She thought of her childhood spent skiing at Sugarloaf, summers sailing off the Maine coast, how beautiful life was, and how much more she wanted to do.

No one saw Grace and Jack as they were enveloped by the wall of snow—death for them, as for most people, was a private matter. But had someone been watching, they would have seen Jack and Grace's mittens ripped off so they could hold hands as they faced the wall of snow moving downslope.

It was a hell of a way to die.

David

Twenty-three Minutes

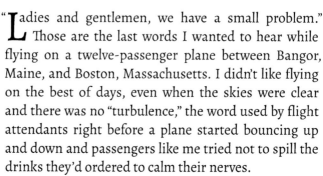

"Ladies and gentlemen, we have a small problem." Those are the last words I wanted to hear while flying on a twelve-passenger plane between Bangor, Maine, and Boston, Massachusetts. I didn't like flying on the best of days, even when the skies were clear and there was no "turbulence," the word used by flight attendants right before a plane started bouncing up and down and passengers like me tried not to spill the drinks they'd ordered to calm their nerves.

"Nancy, the stewardess, will explain what's going on," the captain continued, before signing off to focus attention on whatever the "small problem" was. Nancy proceeded to walk down the aisle, explaining to each of us passengers what the problem was.

"We lost a tire on take-off," she said quietly to me and the woman beside me. "We should be fine, because there are two landing wheels on each side of the plane. We decided to proceed on to Logan Airport, because Logan is better able to deal with emergency landings."

"Emergency landing," I said, my heart in my throat. "What does that mean?"

"It means that you'll see a lot of emergency vehicles on the runway as we're landing. And they put foam on the runways. We should be fine."

Easy for her to say, because she'd been trained to calm down passengers. I hadn't been trained to spend twenty-three minutes—the time she'd estimated it would take to get to Logan—wondering whether this would be the last day of my life.

The woman to my right must have been Catholic. She closed her eyes and clutched her rosary beads the whole time. I decided it wouldn't be a good move to hold her hand, especially since her hands were so sweaty.

The guy across the aisle played the stoic, calmly reading the stock tables in the *Wall Street Journal*. Maybe he wanted to figure out how much money he'd be able to leave his kids if he died.

A young couple at the front of the plane were holding hands and looking into each other's eyes like it was the last time they would. So sad. I bet they had no kids, but they did have parents, no doubt. Think how their parents would feel when they learned about the crash of a small plane coming in to Logan.

As for me, I began praying for all the good people in my life, not my normal go-to mode, but if God was real, then I really needed him right now.

Two minutes left. Clutch time. The small plane was approaching Logan. I could see out the front window of the plane; that's how small it was. There were indeed lots of red lights along the runway, meaning lots of ambulances and fire engines. This was for real. You could almost sense everyone on the plane holding their breath and clutching their arm rests.

One minute. Forty-five seconds. The lights on the runway got brighter as we got closer. I closed my eyes. I didn't want to see whatever there was to see when we landed. This was a hell of a way to die. Away from every-

215

one I cared about. In a small plane at a large airport along with a bunch of strangers.

The woman to my right kept moaning, "Sweet Jesus, be with me now." I hoped sweet Jesus would be with me too. If he saved her, he'd have to save me too.

And then....we landed. As smooth a landing as I'd ever experienced in my life.

"We made it," announced the captain. "Thank you for your patience. And welcome to good old Boston, the home of the bean and the cod, where the Lowells talk to the Cabots, and the Cabots talk only to God."

Everybody laughed. Then some of us cheered. Tears streamed down the face of the woman to my right. "Thank you for your prayers," I said to her softly. "Is your last name Cabot, by any chance?"

She didn't get my quip, I guess, because she just said softly, "God bless you."

"God bless you, too," I said.

We slowly got off the plane, shaking the captain's hand before going down the ramp that had been wheeled up to the exit.

Time to make a few phone calls. After a drink. Or two.

Twenty-seven

Write a story in which the impossible is now possible.

Ani

The Green-Eyed Watcher

"She's a watcher" had been the common refrain among adults after they spent time with Ada. Maybe it was her bright green eyes. As Ada had grown up, she had often wondered what adults meant by describing her as a "watcher." Of course, she watched the world around her—there was so much to pick up on. How a slightly drooping smile would indicate discontent, the way someone held a fork could give insight into their upbringing, the way people presented themselves to the world changed subtly (or not so subtly) based on audience, and even tracking what other people spent their time watching could tell you what a person really cared about.

Watching was a form of listening, and, like listening, it could be done superficially or deeply. Ada was a deep watcher. Her bright green eyes absorbed the world around her. This, perhaps, played a large role in her quiet demeanor. She just didn't feel the need to talk a lot when so much could be learned from watching. Ada had learned to go out of her way to talk, to open up to specific people, but she never gave up her intent watching. She spent lots of time in her head—replaying specific moments to analyze the details of someone's body language, the way the morning light shimmered off frosted trees in the winter, the way her brother's voice lowered in volume and his eyes grew steely when he felt attacked by their parents. It was almost like a game.

Ada would never claim to be that self-aware. That was for others to judge. And she felt that for everything she observed, there were a thousand other things she missed. But this complexity and the sheer magnitude of little things that came together to create the world and experiences around her was what made life interesting.

One day, as Ada sat on the front porch of her apartment watching passersby, she heard a voice pop into her head. *"Deadline coming up but wait, put on shoes and oh my gosh where are my keys...here they are, my hair is a mess, I'm not going to get this job. Will Jack call me tonight? Maybe I could just move in with him. Come on pull yourself together..."* And then Ursula, Ada's roommate, burst through the front door, buttoning a blazer.

"Bye, Ada, wish me luck on this interview," Ursula called over her shoulder as she hopped into her car and sped off.

Ada was taken aback—Ursula hadn't been speaking out loud, had she? No, the voice had clearly been Ursula's but a distant echo. Ada got up and walked down the street. A teenage girl was walking toward her *"Do you think he'll notice me at school today? I should have worn my red shoes; why am I trying to be less visible? Wow my legs are sore from field hockey practice yesterday, will there be a pop quiz in Chem? What's mom going to make for dinner? Are my legs fatter than they used to be?"* Ada smiled at the girl as they passed, the voice fading in her head as she walked on.

This couldn't be, was she listening to people's minds? She went into a nearby grocery store and suddenly her head was filled with different voices:

"Organic's worth the extra cost, right?"

"If John doesn't thank me for dinner again, I'm leaving him."

"Don't buy the ice cream, don't buy the ice cream, you're avoiding sugar, you can do it."

"Mom won't mind if I get a pack of gum with the milk she asked for, it's not that much money...."

Ada felt overwhelmed and quickly left, retreating to a patch of woods on the edge of town. How could this be? She could suddenly hear people's thoughts in her head. Could everyone? No...she couldn't tell anyone. Ursula would think she was crazy, or at least weirder than she already thought. This wasn't supposed to be possible. She sat and watched two blue jays playfully flitting between neighboring trees. She felt herself calm down as she watched the birds...it was quiet. She sat against the base of a white pine tree, watching the orange needles compress on the forest floor beneath her feet.

She didn't know how long she spent there, just watching her breath puff out in front of her in the fresh air. But eventually she got up, feeling pins and needles in her feet and her legs growing stiff. She was worried about hearing people's thoughts—it was certainly an invasion of privacy, could other people do it too? Why did she suddenly have this ability? Most of all she was worried that hearing other people's minds would take away the mystery of life, the mystery she worked so hard to crack day after day as she watched the world unfold around her. She felt tears welling up in her bright green eyes as she walked out of the forest and back into town.

David

Getting that Old Time Religion

I never believed much in prayer. Praying was for church people, you know where those massive black ladies like to wear fancy hats to church and then start screamin' and hollerin' about "the Lawd" for all the world to hear, the louder the better. Then they go home and make heaps of fried chicken and collard greens and black-eyed peas and candied yams and serve it all up with biscuits and gravy. And maybe peach cobbler or chocolate pie for dessert. Those sure were good times.

But that wasn't the problem. The problem was that all these good church people shone bright only that one day: Sunday. The rest of the week they had to go shuffling around doing the bidding of white folks as maids or chauffeurs or shoeshine men and putting their own souls on the shelf. So what good did all that praying do for them really, when you think about it?

I did think about it. I had bigger plans. But then, I was not your typical sixteen-year-old negro boy— or ni***r as the white people often called us or as we ourselves called each other if we were feeling ornery enough. This was back in the year 1968, you see, not long after most places in the south had separate drinking fountains for "whites" and "coloreds." And Alabama was such a place, you better believe it.

I liked to read. And write. And do math problems. My teachers said I was special. Most of my friends said I was a momma's boy. They called me pretty boy or teacher's pet. I didn't care. They could do their thing, I would do mine: I wanted to be a doctor. Not only that, I wanted to go to one of those Ivy League schools I'd read about in books. Well, let's be honest, I wanted to go to Harvard, the best of the best, and that was unheard of back then for any colored kid from anywhere, especially one from a small town named New Hope, just outside Birmingham, Alabama.

So one night I decided to pray real hard to make that dream come true; you know, the Harvard dream. The next morning I was so excited about maybe going to Harvard that I decided to walk to school rather than take that rickety old bus with all those fool kids jammed together. I needed time to think and plan.

And just then along the road, I saw a car parked at the side of the road. There was a white guy in the driver's seat looking at a map. When I walked by, he said, "Excuse me, young man, can you tell me how to get to George Washington Carver High School?" Now that was unusual. What kind of white guy ever said "excuse me" to a colored kid? And sounded respectful at that Also, he talked funny. Not Southern, for sure. Maybe even like he was from one of those states up North.

"I know right where it is, sir," I said, minding my best manners. "In fact, I go to school there. I can direct you right there."

The man seemed relieved as he seemed to be running late. So we started to have a real nice conversation. He asked me what grade I was in and whether I liked school and what I liked to do when I wasn't in school. I guess my answers impressed him enough that he figured I wasn't just a dumb colored kid walking along the side of the road. Maybe he thought I was special, just like my teachers did.

"Do you hope to go to college?" he asked, figuring that I'd be thinking of going to one of those teachers' colleges for black kids.

I felt bold. "Sir, I plan to go to Harvard if they'll let me in. I know I can do it. I've always had straight A's. And everyone says I do well on those standard tests, so those SAT tests shouldn't be too big of a problem."

Suddenly, the man pulled the car over to the side of the road. Then he turned toward me. "Son, do you know why I want to find George Washington Carver High School?" I allowed as how I didn't.

"Well, I work in the admissions office at Harvard, and we're trying to recruit more smart African American kids like you. In fact, you're just the kind of young man we're looking for. You should tell your counselor you want to meet with me. If what you say about your academic record is true, I can take it from there."

And that was how it all began. Fifty years ago. On a warm October day in 1968. Along the side of the road. If I hadn't walked to school that day, I would have never met that guy from Harvard. And I probably wouldn't even have applied there, let alone been accepted. But it all worked out. Not only that, after I graduated from Harvard, I went on to Johns Hopkins Medical School. I went on to have an amazing career as a general practitioner in Baltimore, before semi-retiring back to Birmingham where they needed more people willing to work in family medicine.

You know, it's a funny think about praying. I had never really prayed for anything before that night way back then when I prayed that I would go to Harvard.

Someone heard me, I don't know who, but someone heard me. Ever since then, I've had great respect for the power of prayer. And I sure don't mind those big Sunday picnics after church. I even pray that I'll have enough room for peach cobbler by the time dessert comes around.

Twenty-eight

The smell of chocolate.

Ani

Redolence

As I heated up the dark chocolate chips in the double boiler, and the smell of melting chocolate filled my apartment, I was transported back to a ski trip I took my senior year of college. Nestled away in a cabin in the Chic-Choc Mountains of Canada, we had spent our mornings exploring the snowy forests on skis, the afternoons reading by the fire, and the evenings playing endless rounds of bananagrams. And, of course, we had the nightly tradition of making rich hot chocolate by mixing powdered milk, butter, and melted chocolate chips into hot water. It was a concoction that was only appealing in a backcountry cabin with snow frosting the windows and cold air seeping in through the cracks forcing everyone close to the fire. And each night, as I crawled into my sleeping bag and pulled my hat down over my ears, I would lie watching the flickering light of the fire on the far cabin wall, the smell of melted chocolate still hanging in the air.

Memories fill out the shape of an individual's life, but so often they are forgotten in the everyday. Not necessarily because everyone is living in the present, but because many people are focused on the future. I'm guilty of this, too, but I also feel a deep attachment to memory. I have shoeboxes filled with ticket stubs, receipts, and letters from my childhood. I religiously made a photo album for each year of college and I journaled almost every day. I had watched my grandmother succumb to Alzheimer's in her last five years of life. As she had lost her memory, she had lost her sense of self, and we had all lost her before she had physically passed on. So perhaps I felt like I had to be a steward of my memory because no one else could do it for me.

I loved the act of remembering. For me, songs or albums were often associated with a specific time in my life, and I would listen to them when I wanted to revisit an experience—my summer in Alaska, a cross-country road trip, freshman year of college...Smells could do it, too, and I loved how a distinct smell could practically knock you over with a wave of memories associated with that smell. I could sit for hours, traveling back in time through my memory. Thinking of the ups and downs of life that shaped me and put me where I am today made my heart swell with a happy–sad feeling. Was I too obsessed with the past? I didn't think so. For me, remembering the past made me acutely aware that I was living my future memories in the present. And remembering filled me with gratitude for the people and experiences from my past.

When the chocolate chips had melted, I stirred the chocolate goo into a mug of warm milk and settled onto the couch, pulling a blanket over my feet. I sat, breathing in the smell of chocolate and letting the smell transport me back in time.

David

Torn Between Two Loves

Different smells evoke different memories. Chanel
No 5 reminds me of a certain high school girlfriend
who, dare I say, was graciously forthcoming with her
favors. Woodsmoke reminds me of camping trips with
the Boy Scouts, some of my happiest times. And then
there's chocolate.

The smell of chocolate reminds me of my trip to
Europe in the summer of 1963. And that reminds me
of Catherine Barkely dying and the trading floor at the
London Stock Exchange and Charles Dickens's desk
and Big Billy at Barclays. And it reminds me of my dad,
especially my dad.

Let me explain. I spent the summer of 1963 in
London trying to figure out my life or, at least, the next
steps for my life. If I were feeling low, while there, or
needed more than a pint at a pub, I'd cheer myself up
by buying a few chocolate truffles at Charbonnel et
Walker on Bond Street, London's oldest chocolate shop.

Here was my problem. I loved the magic of the
stock market—always have, always will. I got that gene
from my dad. He started working at Merrill Lynch in
New York right after he got out of Yale. He worked
himself right on up to top management. He taught me
about the workings of the market while other kids' dads

were teaching them how to hit a baseball or dribble a basketball. He had me play the market on paper for a year before he let me invest real money. And I just seemed to have a knack for it, much to his delight. I started an investment club at my high school and, later, at Williams.

But I also loved the magic of words. My mother was a writer. She majored in English at Wellesley and then worked for *Life* magazine in New York. And then she quit that job because she wanted to write books, books that people would buy. And she did. She had a knack for writing mystery novels, and she developed quite a following. She never made a lot of money at it, but she didn't need to. My dad always made enough to give our family a "good life." It turns out that I had a knack for writing stories. So I'd write stories for the family and, later, for my college literary magazine. I even wrote an advice column about investing for my college newspaper.

So, you see, as a young man, I was always torn between my two loves: the stock market and writing. My older sister, Amy, had it easier in terms of charting her life path. She loved animals, and she knew she wanted to be a veterinarian. It was that simple. She's a veterinarian today in Seattle.

Neither parent pushed me in one direction or the other, to their credit. I knew I needed to decide what best fed my soul, not theirs. So I decided to spend the summer after my graduation in London. I would spend part of the time reading (it really to got me when Catherine Barkley died in Hemingway's *Farewell to Arms*), and writing and visiting literary sites, like the Charles Dickens Museum or Daunt Books on Marylebone High Street with its long oak galleries and graceful skylights. And I visited Dad's Yale roommate, Big Billy Brown at Barclays, a major investment firm. Dad had wanted me to learn how the London investment world differed from that in New York.

It was really a great summer, as I look back. Here I was on my very own, for the first time, and I was throwing myself into my two big passions. How could I lose? But I needed to decide whether to start right in at Merrill Lynch—getting a job would be no problem, given my dad's position with the firm—or to take the risk and just start writing. Maybe I'd start as a freelancer. Or maybe tackle a novel. Or write a play. I had saved some money from all my investing, so I could get by for a year or two, for sure.

Finally, with only a week left in the summer, I made the decision: I would take the writing route. Better to start early. I could always invest later. But then, just a day after I had made that decision, I got a phone call. It was my Mom. It didn't sound like her, at first, and I thought it might be the connection. But that wasn't it. Her tone was different because of what she had to tell me. My dad had died of a massive heart attack, just like that, no forewarning. She wanted me to rush right home and help her with all the details. She also wondered if I'd be willing to go into Dad's office and give the news to all his clients. I told her I would, of course.

Hemingway could wait.

Twenty-nine

"There was a ring in his teacup...."

Ani

The Swedish Ring

Noah's official profession was a businessman, but this was really just a front for his work with MI6. Sometimes he wished his life didn't have to be so private—he had to lie to every girlfriend, it was hard to maintain friendships, and even his family had become distant once he started working for the bureau. For the most part, it suited Noah. He didn't really feel the need for other people in his life, but still, sometimes it would be nice to be closer with people, he thought.

Noah was currently in Stockholm where a Viking ring had been stolen from the Nordic Museum. While this wasn't the domain of the British Secret Intelligence Service, the same art thief was believed to be responsible for stealing from the British museum, so SIS had been called. Noah loved Sweden—Stockholm was clean, there was regular *fika* (the beautifully Swedish concept of taking a break, usually with good food and drink), and he loved walking across the bridges that connected the different islands of the Stockholm archipelago. He was currently at a small café in Gamla Stan—the Swedish Old Town—waiting to meet up with Lars, with whom he would be working on the case.

When Lars arrived, they ordered tea and cardamom buns and sat down to go over what they knew. The art thief had previously been caught stealing from one of Oxford's libraries, but the charges had been dropped on a technicality. That had been two years ago. Since then, there had been robberies in major cities across Europe, and the art thief had happened to have been in the vicinity close to the times of the robberies, but there had never been enough evidence to make a case against him. Lars had been involved in these cases with Noah since the beginning.

Noah had never liked Lars, who struck him as impetuous and rash. And he always seemed to treat their cases like a vacation, rushing through the case work so he could hit up some nearby bar or beach or mountain chalet, depending on where they were. And Noah had always felt like Lars was hiding something, which was the nature of being a spy, but still....

This morning was no different. Noah asked Lars routine questions—when had the ring been stolen, had any security alarms gone off, were there security cameras, when had Lars been notified?—at this last question, Noah noticed Lars fidget slightly in his chair. Odd. For the other questions, Lars stated essentially verbatim what had been in the police report. It felt like they were getting nowhere. After an hour of going over the report, Noah got up to go to the bathroom, taking extra time to wash his hands, straighten his shirt, and just breathe. Lars was really starting to get on his nerves.

When he returned to the table, he found Lars gone. Bathroom? Had he stepped outside to take a call? Noah sat, draining the last of the Earl Gray from his teacup. As he did so, he felt something hard knock against his teeth. He spit whatever it was back into the bottom of his cup. It was a ring...*the* ring. He'd spent hours poring over photographs of this ring in the past few days. He looked around but then it hit him. It all made perfect sense—the lack of interest in the cases, the fact that Lars had always gotten to the crime scene before him. Lars wasn't coming back. He must have slipped the ring in Noah's cup before he left. Was he trying to frame him?

Noah looked around ,but knew Lars was gone, probably planning to lie low before his next robbery.

Fuck, Noah thought, as he dialed British SIS.

David

False Alarm

Not many young American men drink tea, but I happen to prefer tea to coffee, even though some people might think I'm a weirdo or a pansy. So I was sitting down to have my tea (licorice spice tea, if you must know) when I noticed something unusual in the bottom of the cup—a ring.

Now this wasn't just an ordinary run-of-the-mill ring. It was the engagement ring I had bought my fiancée, Margie. How the hell had the ring ended up in my tea? That's what I wanted to know. And then I remembered. Margie and I had had a huge fight earlier that day. She said she wondered if we should even get married. She knew I liked my tea, so the riddle was solved: She had put the ring in my favorite teacup as a not-so-subtle way of telling me it was over.

I was shocked, let me tell you. And sad. And pissed. We generally had a fine relationship, all things considered. Oh sure, we argued sometimes. Maybe she wants a man who will always agree with her and not talk back What kind of a relationship is that, I ask you? She didn't have to be so subtle about breaking up with me. What kind of a woman does that? Not any kind of woman I want to marry, that's for sure.

So then I began questioning myself. What had I done wrong? What had she done wrong? Were we both at fault? Could we have worked it out with a little counseling? I had no good answers, and I sure didn't want to get back into the dating scene. Maybe I just wasn't meant to get married. I thought I had found my soul mate, but I guess not.

What had we been arguing about in the first place? To tell you the truth, I couldn't even remember. Must have been some petty little thing. I just sat in my chair for a long time staring at the ceiling with my tea getting cold. Screw the tea. Screw her. Or, more accurately, don't screw her—ever again.

I closed my eyes trying to go to sleep, thinking I'd feel better after a nap, more able to get my life back together. Then I felt a gentle tap on my shoulder. It was Margie. "I'm so sorry, Andy. I didn't mean to. I just lost it."

"That's all right, Margie," I interrupted. "I guess we just weren't mean to be."

"What?" She cried. "What do you mean by that? I'm upset because I misplaced my engagement ring and you're saying that means we shouldn't get married! I don't understand. Please explain."

"Is this what you're looking for," I asked, pointing to the ring in the saucer.

"Oh, my God, you found it!" she screamed. "I've been looking all over for that ring. I took it off to wash the dishes, and I couldn't find it. Are you mad at me?"

"No," I said, "not mad at all. Just kind of relieved."

Thirty

How the hell do these people live like this?

Ani

Racing Time

She gulped down her food before I had finished serving my own plate of salad. I thought back to my family dinners growing up—the agonizing chore of waiting, with a full plate of food in front of me, until everyone had sat down. Back in the day, I would have loved nothing more than to chow down like my life depended on it, but as I stared across the table at my friend's empty plate, I felt a pang of sadness. Was it too much to want to enjoy a nice meal together?

I was twenty-four and living in a small apartment in Seattle with three friends. One I knew from college, and two were lifelong family friends. We had all taken some time post-college to travel and hold different jobs before serendipitously ending up in Seattle for different reasons. I was earning my PhD at UW in environmental and forest sciences. I got to conduct most of my fieldwork in the Hoh rainforest on the Olympic Peninsula. As I moved between trees measuring the diameter, noting different species of moss, and observing leaf herbivory, time slipped away and became irrelevant. I was totally engrossed in the feel of the bark under my hands or the movement of my feet as I navigated roots and downed branches. The immediate sense of purpose tethered me to the present in a way I rarely felt in other situations.

Returning to my apartment at the end of a day in the field was always a shock to my system. My roommates, two of whom worked in tech and one of whom was just constantly on the prowl for the next fellowship to apply for, always seemed to be racing against time. From eating dinner in less than ten minutes to frantically scouring the apartment for a lost item, our world at home felt fast-paced and frenetic. I longed for space to sit and drink coffee while watching the sky lighten over the Seattle skyline, or to light a candle with dinner and sit and talk until conversation dried up, or to stretch my legs out on the couch with a book, unconcerned with the time of day....

My project assistant, Erik, approached life slowly. Transitions always seemed to take him double the time that they should, yet I loved watching him as he checked over field equipment, ensured the lab machines were properly shut off, and filed away experiment notes and scientific papers. He was always so focused, so present...I had always thought of myself as an efficient person, despite my appreciation for the "little things" in life. But Erik made me want to slow down more. And I found his meticulous and focused inefficiency intriguing and—if I'm being honest—quite attractive.

Some people go through life racing against time, while others seem to slow time down. When I was with Erik or in the Hoh rainforest, time slowed down. I had room to breathe, to think, to question. As I continued to glare across at my roommate's empty plate (I hadn't even taken a bite yet!) I felt something give inside of me. How the hell do people live like this? Where's the joy in life if you're not moving slowly enough to look around you? As I picked at my food, while my roommates got up from the table and began to clean up around me, I resolved that tomorrow I would begin looking for a new apartment. I wanted to live alone.

David

A Fish Out of Water

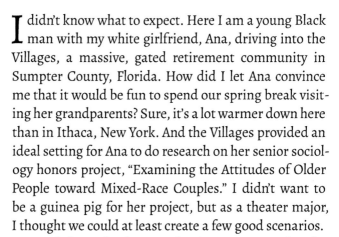

I didn't know what to expect. Here I am a young Black man with my white girlfriend, Ana, driving into the Villages, a massive, gated retirement community in Sumpter County, Florida. How did I let Ana convince me that it would be fun to spend our spring break visiting her grandparents? Sure, it's a lot warmer down here than in Ithaca, New York. And the Villages provided an ideal setting for Ana to do research on her senior sociology honors project, "Examining the Attitudes of Older People toward Mixed-Race Couples." I didn't want to be a guinea pig for her project, but as a theater major, I thought we could at least create a few good scenarios.

It didn't take long to begin our research: The uniformed guard at the entrance stared long and hard at both of us while he was calling Ana's grandparents to see if it was okay if he let us in. We weren't the "normal" visitors, it seemed.

After we passed that test, we learned why a snarky reporter once described "The Villages" as "the place where some old white Midwesterners retire to play shuffleboard and attend happy hours before they die." Or, more recently, "Trumpland with a Viagra Chaser."

"How the hell do these people live like this?" I asked Ana.

"I have no idea," she said sheepishly. "Maybe they just want to be around their own kind."

"Well, I said, They might not want to be around my kind—or you, for that matter, if you're mixed up with my kind."

"Just relax," she begged, "Let's try to make the most of this week."

And make the most of it is what we did. We spent one long afternoon at the Tiki Bar, tossing down rum punches with the old people. They seemed nervous with us there, at first, but they slowly loosened up. I thought, "What the hell, I'm going to liven this place up," and I began singing Harry Belafonte's classic, "The Banana Boat Song." Most of the people around the bar knew that song and they began singing along with me.

We even tried our hand at shuffleboard, entering a mixed pair competition. We were the most mixed pair there, to say the least. Anyway, we came in third out of sixteen pairs, which was not bad considering that neither of us had played before.

Ana conducted some informal interviews with people about the mixed-race matter. Most of them seemed okay with the idea, although a few people got very nervous when she brought up the topic. After the first two days, the word had gotten out that Ana was visiting her grandparents and that her boyfriend was, well, me. Happily, the word had also been passed, because of our Tiki Bar singing and shuffleboard performance, that we were good people. I guess we passed the test.

Something else happened during that week. We became friendly with the three couples that Ana's grandparents had invited over for cocktails. After some small talk—I much prefer real, get-down-and-dirty talk—we began sharing our lives with these people. They wanted to know what it was like to be in college these days. And whether we faced any discrimination because we were a mixed-race couple. I asked them about their lives and careers, always a fascinating topic with me. I think we all grew from these interactions; at least, I know I did.

I also really liked Ana's grandparents, Pam and Jesse. They were warm, relaxed and friendly—not at all what I had expected them to be. On the last day, they urged us to visit us again the following year. Back in our bedroom, Ana asked me, "What do you think? Should we come back next year?"

"Sure," I said, "but please leave your reporter's pad at home next spring. Let's not play the Margaret Mead game. Let's just kick back and be us."

"Sounds like a good idea," she said, relieved about how everything had turned out.

Reflections

Whew! That was fun. Here are some of my reflections after partnering with Ani Williams to take a romp through flash fiction.

1. It's great to be able to write something out of whole cloth, not being chained to "the facts," as I have been throughout my entire career, during which I wrote promotional materials for colleges and profiles for newspaper and magazines.
2. In some cases, Ani took a totally different approach; at other times, our efforts were eerily similar. (We never read the other person's work until we had each written our own.)
3. I never really understood writers of fiction when they said that sometimes the characters take over, and the writer just goes along for the ride. That happened often with me. Also, I might start a story with one ending in mind and then change directions in the middle of the story.
4. Some differences did occur because of our vast fifty-seven-year age gap. Ani didn't know about some of the cultural references I included. And I, of course, am not as tuned in to how a younger person sees the world.

5. At one point, I worried that Ani might be upset with some of the sleazy characters I created, like the oil executive who had a mistress on the side. But her story to that same prompt started with the F-word so I figured that a little seaminess was okay.

6. During the project, I began reading more fiction with a focus on how the author thought through the whole process—developing the character's viewpoint, creating a realistic sense of place, and keeping the story moving along.

7. The internet is terrific for digging up good specific details to help a story come alive.

8. I felt more and more comfortable with each new prompt. In fact, I really looked forward to getting down to business each time a new prompt arrived.

9. Ani's storytelling seemed to become more confident and fluid as we went along.

As a final reflection, I'm not sure where I'll go from here with my writing. But I do know that I'll feel more confident about tackling something in the fiction realm—a short story or a play or a novel. And I also know that I'll have even greater appreciation for the seasoned fiction writers who are so skilled at, to put it crudely, "just making stuff up." I salute them.

Thank you, Ani, for suggesting this idea and for being such a fine partner as we romped together through the fields of flash fiction.

—*David Treadwell*

My flash fiction exchange with David provided the backdrop to an adventurous and formative fall of 2020. From sitting on my patio in Central Washington's hot September sun and writing one of my first stories, to getting up early while staying in Nederland, Colorado, to write, only to become distracted by a moose walking by my window, for me the stories not only captured a specific idea from my imagination, but they are also grounded in different places I lived this fall and different people I was lucky enough to spend time with. The year 2020 was a time of considerable learning in many ways. As I faced an unprecedented remote year of college, became distanced from friends and family, engaged with the Black Lives Matter movement, felt the many losses of COVID-19, dealt with the uncertainty of a tanking economy, and navigated a politically tumultuous landscape leading up to the 2020 presidential election, I found myself working hard to practice resilience and find joy in the everyday, even if some days that felt like the hardest task in the world. And so I think that, while all of these stories are fictitious, each holds nuggets of the truth and reflects emotions or tensions

I was wrestling with at different points throughout the fall of 2020.

David and I made certain to never read the other person's story for a given prompt until we had written and sent our own. It always felt like such a treat to finally open his story and see how he had approached the same prompt. Sometimes we found we had eerily similar stories, and other times they could not have been more different. It was interesting to reflect on how our differences in age and life experience (and, of course, his more robust writing history) influenced how we approached a prompt. We also laughed at prompts that one of us found particularly easy, while the other struggled to address them. As a result of sharing our stories with each other and writing in response to the same prompts, I became much more aware of how much our own experiences shape our writing, even when that writing is fictitious. And, by designing this project as an exchange, we were both able to honor our strengths while also honing our weaker skills.

My school career has mostly focused on analytical and scientific writing, so this project also pushed my growth as a writer. Early on, I approached my stories like I would any school assignment—an outline with a detailed plan for the beginning, middle, and end. Fiction proved to be a whole different ball game. I wanted to shape my stories to fit a mold I created in my head, and I think this approach often led to clunky, unsatisfying writing. I found that my best stories were often the ones that almost seemed to write themselves. These were the stories that I didn't know the ending of when I sat down to write; rather, I created the characters and setting, and then they ultimately directed their own fate, and I just tried to write fast enough to get it all down.

David was instrumental in providing feedback—asking me questions about certain story elements, praising the strengths of a story, noting my weaknesses, laughing at my general avoidance of dialogue. And I also learned about writing through reading his stories and identifying elements I liked or ways in which he made a character seem three-dimensional (an impressive feat in stories that are often less than a thousand words).

The year 2020 was a big moment in history in different ways, and I have no doubt that most people will have strong memories associated with it. I feel grateful that this flash fiction project with David is one of my memories of 2020. Not only did it allow me to learn from a more skilled writer, it also gave me a creative outlet, provided routine during an uncertain time, and was an excellent opportunity to learn more about the art of writing.

—*Anneka Williams*

About the Authors

DAVID TREADWELL is a professional writer who spent his career writing admissions and fundraising materials for colleges and schools around the country. He writes a weekly column ("Just a Little Old") for the *Times Record*, the local paper in Brunswick, Maine. His interests include reading, theater, walking, mentoring Bowdoin students, and discussing the meaning of life with friends.

ANNEKA WILLIAMS grew up in Vermont's Mad River Valley. She loves reading, running, drinking tea, hiking, gardening, skiing, listening to audiobooks, swimming in the river, woodworking, playing games, and getting up early to watch sunrise. Her favorite books include Anthony Marra's *A Constellation of Vital Phenomena*, Stephen King's *Mr. Mercedes* trilogy, and Rainer Maria Rilke's *Letters to a Young Poet*.